©Christopher Dauth

Sarah Brill began writing for the theatre at the age of 15. She attended four National Young Playwrights Workshops before graduating to the National Playwrights Conference in 1994 with her play *Who the Fuck is Erica Price*. *Who the Fuck is Erica Price* was later produced for Artrage, the Perth Fringe Festival, in 1996. In 1998 Sarah worked as a writer in residence with Salamanca Theatre Company on the production of *Reality Check* and in 2000 wrote a commissioned play for them entitled *Super Serious*. She has had two radio plays produced by the ABC, *BORED* in 1997 and *See* in 2001. In 1999 she was awarded a two year mentorship through Playworks.

GLORY

Sarah Brill

SPINIFEX

Spinifex Press Pty Ltd
504 Queensberry Street
North Melbourne, Vic. 3051
Australia

women@spinifexpresss.com.au
http://www.spinifexpress.com.au

First published 2002
Copyright © Sarah Brill

Cover design by Deb Snibson, Modern Art Production
Group
Typeset in Stone Informal by Palmer Higgs Pty Ltd
Printed and bound by McPherson's Printing Group

National Library of Australia
Cataloguing-in-Publication data:
Brill, Sarah, 1971– .
   Glory.

For secondary school age students.
ISBN 1 876756 25 X.

1. Self-esteem in adolescence – Fiction. 2. Family –
Fiction. 3. Teenagers - Suicidal behavior - Fiction. I.
Title.

A823.4

to Eloise
where ever she may be

and to my sister Deborah
who never gave up

One

I'm standing on a cliff. Below me I can see the ocean. Its waves crashing onto the rocks. It's so far away I think it's a toy. Unreal.

Behind me are my parents and younger sister. They're sitting on the blanket eating the picnic my mother has prepared.

But I am standing. Standing at the edge of a cliff watching the waves crash below.

My mother calls out to me. Probably something like 'come and sit with us, have some food'. But I never hear her voice. The wind carries it away before it reaches my ears. I like that.

I put my toes over the edge of the cliff. I'm trying to feel the fear, the danger. I feel nothing. I hang my whole foot over. Still no fear, no danger. Instead a small amount of power.

I look back at my family. Still eating on that ugly old blanket. I look past them and see the car, the road we arrived by. In my mind I see the path we took from home to here. I know everything behind me. I look back at my family. They look happy together. Complete without me. My mother is laughing at my sister, she has done or said something amusing. My father is reaching for the camera.

I turn my attention back to the cliff. The water that goes on and on and I have no idea where it ends. I look at the waves below me. They are no longer crashing. Instead they are curling around the rocks. Inviting me to join them.

I jump.

Now I'm scared.

The fat girl gets out of her hospital bed and goes to where her family is. They sit in a row on the hard plastic waiting chairs, their faces filled with anxiety. The fat girl goes to those faces and slaps each one: father, sister, mother. Then she laughs because she is strong and because she has done something they never thought she could. As the fat girl walks away from her family, down the hospital corridor, she trips and falls on her face. Her family laughs at her because she looks like a fool and because she is alive.

When she opens her eyes she is lost. The smell is wrong, the bed is wrong. She looks to her right. Her father sits at her side. She looks to her left. Her mother stands at the window. She closes her eyes. Behind her eyes there is nothing. Just black. The black is nice. She knows the black.

As she slowly regains consciousness, over days, hours, minutes, she sees she is in hospital. She opens her eyes to glimpse the scenes around her bed. At first it is light, movement. Shadows against the wall. Then it is her parents, holding her hand, telling her of the house, the neighbours. They tell her everything is going to be all right now. She doesn't understand what they're trying to say. She closes her eyes.

They were born one year apart. Her mother was tired all the time and the new baby just slept. She was left to her own devices. The new baby was fed on the breast, she was always given a bottle. At first she tried to share her mother's breast with the new baby but her mother wouldn't let her.

Later she realised it was because she wasn't her real mother. Only real mothers could give their real babies the breast. You had to be a perfect match. If she were a real baby, her real mother would have given her the breast. But she wasn't and she had to make do with the bottle.

Often she opens her eyes to darkness. No family in her room. Just the soft shuffle of a nurse walking nearby. The sounds of people trying to sleep or of people sleeping. The nurse walks into her room. She quickly closes her eyes.

Nothing they can say makes sense to her as she lies in her hospital bed. She becomes aware of her pain and begins to wonder what they're doing in her room. It seems rude to her that they are there. She closes her eyes, tries to shut them out, but that seems rude too. It's rude for her to shut them out and rude of them to be there, intruding on her pain.

It's hard for a mother to watch her daughter, lying there like that. Harder when the mother doesn't understand why. It's hard for a mother to watch her daughter in pain and not be able to help. I don't understand, the mother says as she rocks her head in her hands, I just don't understand. Her husband is calm and soothing but he doesn't understand either. So they attend the hospital every day and listen to the doctors. They hold their daughter's hand and they try to think positively. But the mother, she watches her daughter on the hospital bed and she starts to think it's her fault the daughter is in that bed.

She lies in her hospital bed and she thinks about dying. She imagines her death and sees that it could be beautiful. She lives for her pain now. It wakes her up in the morning and keeps her awake through the night, until finally, in the early hours of the morning when her body can't take any more, she falls asleep knowing she will wake up to her pain again. Her pain becomes her glory. In it she knows she is alive and in it she feels like she is dying.

Sometimes she gets scared. When she looks into the eyes of her parents and sees their fear. Then it becomes too real. She is dying. There is nothing they can do to stop her. She worries she won't be able to control her own death. That it will be ugly. But the pain takes over her thoughts and she relaxes into it. She holds on to her glory and nothing can touch her there.

The father watches his daughter lying in her hospital bed and he is angry. So angry that this has happened to his daughter, to his family, to him. He doesn't know who to blame. Where the fault lies. It is easy to say it is them. They did something wrong. He can't remember doing anything wrong. And the sick daughter, so still on her bed. So quiet. He wants to push her for answers, shake her until she is forced to tell him why. He believes if he knows, if he understands, then his anger will go away. But they have agreed not to push her into telling them anything. To let her speak in her own time. So the father must watch his daughter in her hospital bed without questions, trying to push his anger away.

She lies in her hospital bed and holds onto her glory. She is sick. Sicker than she has ever been in her life. She feels it in every part of her body. They say she burnt herself from the inside out. She doesn't remember. They say she drank her parents out of cleaning products. She doesn't remember. They ask her why she did it. Was she trying to kill herself? Did she want to die? She says she can't remember doing it, how can she explain why. They go away. But she knows they'll be back the next day. And they are.

She was found in a basket on the doorstep. Only one day old. Wrapped in a white blanket with a small pink rabbit that had hand stitched eyes. She was crying. That's how they knew she was there. And there was a note, pinned to her blanket. It explained how her mother loved her but couldn't keep her. It said, 'Please look after my baby'.

When she tells this story to a friend and one of her parents hears her they tell her it really wasn't like that. They tell a story of legal proceedings and waiting and piles of paperwork. But she isn't interested in this version of her story. It's boring. She likes to think of herself in the basket. One day old. And her real mother, crying as she walked away.

They come back with a social worker, a child psych-ologist. They come back with more questions. They want her to play games, tell stories. She doesn't. She tells them she can't. She's too sick. The truth is she can't remember how to play games or if she knows any stories. She doesn't want to think about why she's here and she's not interested in sharing her dreams with a stranger. She only cares about her glory. Keeping her glory safe so that no one can take it away.

Her parents visit every day. They don't ask her to ex-plain. They talk of other things. They talk of the world outside the hospital. She has no interest in what they say. But she listens. And she smiles. In her smile she is saying, look at me, I'm trying. And her parents go home feeling a little better. She realises a smile will only satisfy them for so long, but at this stage, with all her energy focused on her glory, she has nothing else to offer.

She has just come home from a party. A bad party. She hears the car that dropped her off, drive away and she sinks to the floor. She can't remember why she had a bad time. Something in the eyes of strangers and the words of friends. Something in her head. She has had a bad time. She stands slowly and makes her way through the house. She is running her hands through her hair, dragging her nails along the wall. She is reaching, clutching at objects, tearing at her hair. She is in the kitchen, gorging herself, not from the fridge but from the cupboard under the sink. From the laundry. From the bathroom. Tasting, tearing, swallowing anything that will hurt. She is in the toilet vomiting. She is on the floor crying. She cannot remember why she had a bad time.

And then the pain begins to fade. Her body is healing itself. Working against her the way it always does. And her parents are smiling more and the doctors are talking of restricted diets but saying she'll be fine. She doesn't feel fine. She's losing her glory. She hits at her stomach, where she knows it will hurt the most. Her arms are weak, she can't hit hard. But she continues as long as she can and she gets her glory back.

The nurses find the bruises on her stomach. They strap her arms to the bed. They feed her with a spoon. She refuses to eat. She says she is too fat, lying on the bed, not doing any exercise. She says she doesn't need to eat. The nurses laugh at her and force the food down her throat.

Sometimes her sister is there, dressed in her school uniform, quietly watching. Her parents haven't told her what happened. She just knows it was bad. That she's lucky to still have an older sister. They never speak. Both unsure what to say.

Sister, lying in your bed, looking so weak. I have never spent so much quiet time with you sister, so much time where you have not told me to leave or made fun of me until I do. My sister, says the sister, but only inside her head. My sister, listen to me. Your eyes are closed but I want you to listen to me. Don't be afraid to come home. It's not the same without you and you have been gone for so long. Our parents barely speak now and I can't stand to sit at the table with them. Sister, they say if you try, if you try just that little bit harder you can come home. You can come home really soon. Sister, they say you are not trying.

A doctor will often come into her room. A doctor who tells her she's going to be fine and next time not to be so silly. A cheerful doctor who tires her with questions. Does it hurt here? Here? Here? And the doctor pokes around her body until she has to say it hurts everywhere. Everywhere. And the doctor looks worried and wonders whether she should be given pain killers. But she says no. Pain killers will reduce what little glory she has left.

Everyone tells her she's going to be fine. They tell her things are going to be different when she is well, and she will be well. She can't remember how things were. Who she was. She doesn't understand. She tries to ask her parents, the doctor. They tell her it doesn't matter. She just has to concentrate on getting well. But she doesn't understand. She doesn't know how.

They tell him her feelings of insecurity have something to do with her adoption but he can't understand that because he was adopted and he considers it the best thing that ever happened to him. He loved his adoptive parents and always knew they loved him. He felt like they had rescued him from something terrible. He didn't know what. He didn't want to know what. He was just grateful they were there. He suggested they adopt when it looked like it might be hard for them to have children of their own. And he was excited when they agreed to do it. He wanted to do for another child what his parents had done for him. He thought they had.

She lies in her bed and searches for that small ball of glory left somewhere in her body. When she finds it she rolls it around, tries to make it bigger. She lets her glory tell her stories, sing her songs, rock her to sleep. But when she wakes up it is with dreams she doesn't understand and memories she can only half recall. And it is without her glory.

She is resigned to the loss of her glory. Lying in her bed with her arms strapped to her sides is too much. She will not allow herself to be fed like a baby. She must let her glory go this time and hope that some-how, soon, she'll get it back.

She has become a part of the hospital routine, lying in her bed. A permanent fixture. She hasn't had the courage to ask how long she has been here. She knows it has been more than a while. She can tell by the length of her sister's hair.

At night she listens to the nurses talk. They talk to pass the night hours and they are well practised. The nurses talk without fear of who may hear and what the consequences may be. As she listens she tries to give faces to the endless stream of names, she tries to create lives for the faces. But the names she doesn't know blend with the faces she remembers. She becomes so confused that she has to stop herself from thinking. Instead she concentrates on the nurses' words. One word at a time until she falls asleep.

One night a nurse sees she is still awake, knows she is listening to their conversation. A child with adult ears, she says as she fusses around the bed and she knows not what to make of the comment. So she says nothing and the nurse simply shrugs and goes back to the conversation in the hall. What else is there to do. She can't pretend she hasn't heard. They are talking about one of the nurses who has just had an abortion. The nurse works in a different area so she doesn't know her, not her face. But she knows about the abortion. She knows the boyfriend never even knew there was a pregnancy and that the nurses think that was wrong.

She's never had a boyfriend. Not really. Never had sex. She can't imagine what it would be like. The nurse's abortion is just another event around her that she doesn't really understand. She wonders what it would feel like. How it would compare to the pain she has been feeling. If there would be any glory. Or would it be more of a loss. She was only a baby when her mother was pregnant with her sister. She doesn't remember anything, except a general feeling of excitement that something good was coming and a feeling of dread that everything was going to change.

They begin to talk of home. They say things like, if you eat all of your dinner you'll be able to go home soon. If you take this medicine, if you promise to be a good girl … She's not sure she wants to go home.

She tries to remember what it's like. She pictures her room and walking from the bathroom to the kitchen. It doesn't seem real. She can't even think about school. It makes her head spin, her stomach churn.

She has had a relapse, they say. You do understand. No. No, I don't understand. She was so well. She was going to come home. I don't understand. She will still go home, they say. Just not as soon as we thought. And they talk and they talk and still she doesn't understand. She is her mother. She knows her daughter better than any of these people who keep asking her if she understands. She sees herself standing up and saying I am her mother, you do understand, don't you? She is my daughter and I'm taking her home. But she remains sitting. She feigns an understanding and says, so when do you think she'll be able to come home?

They say she is sick again. One of her organs is in trouble, failing. She can't feel anything. When they told her what was going on she thought it might be her glory. She thought her glory was coming back to her. But she can't feel anything. The doctors aren't too worried. Just a little set back they say. You'll be home before you know it.

She doesn't want to hear those words. That word. Home. Home means she would live in her parents' house. She would walk to school every morning. Walk home every night. They say this word over and over. They hold it above her head like a threat, thinking it a treat. No, she's not ready to go home, she has only just got used to the hospital.

I thought you wanted to come home.

I do mum. She lies. What else can she do?

Well, I understand of course. The doctors have explained. She lies. What else can she do. *But we miss you. And we'd like to you be home with us.*

I'm sure I'll be able to come home soon.

The doctors feel you could be trying harder.

I am trying, it's just …

What is it? Is it school? You don't have to go back right away. Whenever you're ready.

No. It's not school.

Then … ?

I don't know. And she doesn't. Not in words.

Well, the mother gives up, *when you're ready then.*

She knows her time is nearly up. She is running out of excuses. Her body failing her as always, this time not with inefficiency but with its skill at healing itself. She didn't think, after what she'd done, that it could be so strong. The doctor comes to look at her chart. She confirms her fear.

Looks like we'll be saying goodbye to you soon.

Yes.

Well that's good, isn't it?

Pause.

Isn't it?

Yes.

The doctor moves closer, as if to get a better look at her face. She sits beside her.

Would you like to talk about going home? About what could happen when you leave?

But she doesn't want to talk. She doesn't want to talk about anything. She doesn't want to think about anything. Because she doesn't know anything. She feels like everything she has known in the past is gone. All she has is the hospital bed, the hospital room, the hospital routine.

And then the routine changes. Cherie moves into her ward. She hasn't had to share her room before. She's been too sick, too difficult. At first she is resentful. This is her room, her hospital, her routine. In her last few days of clinging to what she knows, some one else will change everything. But she has to admit to herself that she's getting bored. That she knows the routine so well it has become too small to fill her days. Now she has something to watch. Someone else to think about. Someone with a name

17

and a face that she's not supposed to remember. Someone who's sick, like her. She gets curious.

Cherie is a thin girl. She looks a few years older, although it's hard to tell, and she has bandages up both arms. When she is wheeled into the room the nurse introduces them and then leaves. They both lie silently in the room.

I fell over and accidentally slit both my wrists.
What?
You've been staring at me ever since I got here.
I'm sorry.
I don't care.
Must've hurt.
I said I don't care.

When Cherie's mother comes to visit her she draws the curtains around her bed. The voices are soft and muffled. She doesn't stay long but when she leaves the curtains remain around the bed. When her family come to visit they leave the curtains open. She doesn't ask them not to. They don't stay long either. After all this time there is little to say. They ask her about Cherie and comment that it will be nice for her to have some company. She doesn't tell them about their conversation. After her family leave the nurse comes in and pulls the curtains back from around Cherie's bed. Cherie picks up a magazine and reads like there's no one else in the room.

She likes having Cherie in the room, even though she ignores her. It gives her something else to think about. For the first time she can remember since she's been in the hospital she's thinking about someone else's problems. She wants to know what happened. Maybe she really did fall. She wants to know if she feels the same things about being in the hospital and imagines she does. She imagines them talking. Revealing their inner secrets and becoming best friends. They would be soul sisters and tell each other everything. Then she listens to her own thoughts and knows they're stupid. So she stays silent and hopes Cherie will start a conversation.

So what's your name then?
Anne.
Silence.
Cherie.
I know.
How long have you been here then?
Few months.
How many months?
Four.
Long time.

Yeah.

I just got here.

I know.

Cherie goes back to her magazine. She doesn't speak for the rest of the day.

In the morning Cherie is visited by the hospital psychiatrist. They take a walk out of the ward. When Cherie returns she's on her own and she's crying. She lies on her bed and listens to Cherie crying. She imagines herself going over there, putting an arm around her. She imagines how that would stop the crying and how Cherie would look up to her and smile, her face damp with tears. Then she imagines another scene. A scene where Cherie pushes her away and she is left standing there. Her arm, her thoughts of comfort, useless. So she remains in her bed, listening to Cherie cry.

It's dark when she wakes up. At first she doesn't know why she's awake and then she feels the tugging at her arm. She turns around. Cherie stands by her bed dressed in her nightgown. She motions for her to be quiet and to follow. She hesitates. Cherie pulls at her arm until she finds herself out of bed and following Cherie down the corridor. They run quietly through the hospital until they reach a set of double doors. Cherie doesn't stop. She pushes the doors open and begins to climb the stairs. But she can't go on. She has to stop and catch her breath. Cherie realises she is climbing alone and looks back at her.

Come on!

She begins to climb the stairs again, trying to remember how long it has been since she did this much exercise. All that time, just lying in the bed. They never encouraged her to do much. The occasional walk down the hall maybe. She tries to remember what has been said. She wants to know whose fault it is. Did they tell her she should be doing exercise? Did she ignore their advice? She can't remember.

By the time she reaches the top of the stairs she has decided it is the fault of the doctors and staff. No one ever told her to exercise. No one ever thought to mention it. She walks out of the stairwell to find she is on the roof of the hospital. Cherie is lying on her back staring up at the sky.

Thought you'd never make it.
Me too.
You've been in that bed too long.
I know.

Cherie falls silent. She doesn't know what to do. She

sits down beside her. Looks at Cherie. Looks at the sky. The night sky is clear and bright with a half moon. She had forgotten what it felt like to see the moon.

It's nice up here.

Yeah.

How did you know where to find it?

Just wandering around one night.

But you've only been here two days.

Before.

They fall into silence again.

So why did you do it?

What?

You know.

Cherie points to her wrists.

I didn't.

It doesn't matter how you did it.

How do you know?

They always put us together.

Us?

Us suicidals. You don't have to tell me. I don't really care.

Why did you bring me up here?

You looked like you needed a change of scene.

Cherie pulls a small flask from her pocket. She takes

a swig and then offers it. It's scotch. She's not allowed to drink scotch. Before she was too young and now her body can't take it. All that sugar. Alcohol is on her list of things she can never put into her body. Alcohol, sugar, chocolate, anything that requires a bit of digestion. They're all on her list.

She takes the flask and has a small sip. She feels it burning down her insides and knows she'll be sick the next day. They stay on the roof as long as they think they can get away with it. They take turns to sip from the flask. As they creep back to their beds Cherie starts to laugh. She has to stuff her hand in her mouth to stop the noise coming out. Looking at Cherie with her hand in her mouth makes her laugh too. When they get back to their room they have to put pillows over their faces to stop the noise. She doesn't know whether it's the scotch or the fear of getting caught by the nurses that's making her laugh. She doesn't really care. She's just happy to be laughing.

The next day is spent with secret glances passed between the two girls. She doesn't feel as bad as she should after the scotch. Maybe the list is wrong. They say little, but occasionally one will start to giggle and this is quickly followed by the other joining in. They muffle their laughter on the pillows or with their hands. She hopes that Cherie will take her to the roof again.

When her parents come to visit they are impressed by how well she looks. She didn't think to try to hide it and begins to regret her good spirits. Cherie, on the other hand, continues to giggle. Her parents' eyes start to wander across the ward to where Cherie's bed is. They return their gaze to her as she lies in her bed trying to look sick and unhappy. Trying not to laugh.

After her parents leave they spend the rest of the day together. Like friends. They play cards and flick through magazines. They try to do a crossword puzzle but give up after a short time. They talk about the nurses. She tells Cherie about the abortion. They don't talk about themselves, about why they are here. Cherie doesn't ask her questions like she did on the roof and she is relieved. On the roof perhaps she could have told her even though she didn't. But down here, in their ward, she wants to pretend they are friends. And friends, she thinks to herself, don't need to explain.

That night she sleeps quietly. She assumes Cherie does the same. In the morning she looks over to Cherie's bed and finds the curtains are pulled around. They remain this way for the rest of the day.

It makes her realise how bored she has been in the hospital now that she is forced to spend the day alone. And yet, even as the hours drag through the day, she knows she is not ready to leave.

The doctor thinks otherwise.

You're going home on Friday.
Friday?
There's nothing more we can do for you here.
But I don't feel well enough to go home.
Well you are. Okay?

She nods. What else can she do.

When her parents arrive for their daily visit they are excited by the news. Her father comments on being glad to never see the inside of this place again and she feels insulted. The inside of this place is her home. She doesn't want to exchange it for some-where else. Somewhere they say she belongs even though she knows she doesn't. She's always known she doesn't belong there. But she doesn't say any of this. She doesn't tell her father he has insulted her. She remains quiet, says she is tired and begins to hope they leave soon.

Thursday night comes too quickly. She has with-drawn from Cherie since they told her she was leaving. It doesn't make much difference, Cherie has withdrawn from her too. She doesn't understand why but she assumes it is tied to the bandages on her arms, to why she is here. Occasionally they throw comments to each other across the room. She will complain about the food and Cherie will complain about the nurses. She hasn't said she is leaving. On Friday she will be gone. As unexpected as Cherie's arrival.

My family are talking inside my head.

I don't want anyone to talk about it when she comes home.

My mother.

Why?

My sister.

I think it best not to upset her.
But why?
Because I think it will be best.
What if she brings it up?
I think your mother is suggesting we all try not to upset your sister when she gets home.

My father.

Yes. We all need to do our best to make her feel at home. And there's to be no talk of food.

Okay.

I'm sure if we all work together we can make it a happy homecoming.

Okay.

Is that all dear? I really do have to get going.

Of course dear. Have a nice day.

Her mother has drawn up her list in large print and stuck it on the fridge. The list is of things she can't eat and things she should eat. Looking at the list makes her not want to eat at all. It's not a list for a week or a month or until she is better. She looks at the list and knows that this is her list for life.

My family are talking in front of my face.

Dinner time!

Come on everyone hurry up. You must be starving.

It's so nice to have you home.

Is that all you're eating? Don't you think ...

This is fine. Thank you.

Everyone stares at my plate. My mother's first attempt at cooking from my list.

So what did you do today?

I don't know. Just sort of hung around.

Everyone watches my first mouthful.

Watched the tellie hey?

A little.

So, what do you think you'll do next week?

I'm not sure.

Everyone watches my second mouthful.

I was just thinking about school. Of course take as much time as you want, it's just that you've missed so much ...

I'm just not sure ... I don't feel ready yet.

My fork lies on the plate.

Well, you take all the time you need.

I really don't think you should leave it too long though dear. Goodness knows what you've missed and ...

Everyone stares at my fork.

I don't feel ready to go yet.

I take my third mouthful, make it large. Chew carefully.

Well, I'm sure that's fine. How about you missy, how was your day at school?

It was all right.

Is that all?

We got our test back in maths.

And?

I did okay. Can I go to a party on the weekend?

Whose party?

A girl at school.

We'll talk about it later.

Why can't we talk about it now?

Because I said we'll talk about it later.

This is great dear. Isn't it girls?

Yes.

Great.

Well, I'm not sure how you can tell, you've both hardly touched it.

Careful scrutiny of my plate.

I'm not very hungry.

The doctor said it was important for you to eat a good sized meal.

And she said it was important that no one pressure me.

We're not pressuring you dear, we're just worried about you.

Well, I'm fine, thank you.

Where are you going?

The days at home are long and boring. She doesn't want to go back to school yet. She keeps saying, I'm not ready. And she isn't. Nothing feels right. She expects that one day it will all snap back. It will be like before the hospital, and she tries to remember how that was.

Her best friend from school rang but she wouldn't speak to her. She told her mother she wasn't ready, and her mother didn't understand. She never expected her to but what would she say after four months in hospital? What would they have to talk about? She wants to put off talking to anyone from school until she's worked out what to say.

She finds it annoying being with her mother all day, her family all night. At the hospital they would leave. They would come at a scheduled time and then they would leave. At home they are there all the time. Always asking her how she is. She always replies I'm not ready yet, thinking it best to refuse all questions, not just the hard ones.

She spends her days wandering around the house. Sometimes she helps her mother or attempts to do the school work her sister brings home for her. She thinks about her glory, and about where it might have gone. She thinks about how she might get it back. She remembers having it, encased in her body. She remembers how it felt, the strength it gave her. She thinks if she had her glory, then she could go to school, answer questions and live in this house, with this family.

It's hard now that her daughter is home. She looked forward to it so much. She was tired of going to the hospital every day, sitting in those awful chairs. She was desperately waiting for her daughter to come home. She thought if she got her daughter home everything would be all right. Or if not all right, better.

Now that she is here she realises how hard it is going to be. They are all creeping around. Trying not to upset her, no one really knowing what to say. She wants to lock anything dangerous away from her. Like when she was learning to crawl. She knows this is pointless. She can't stop her daughter from harming herself, she's old enough to go out and buy anything she wants. If she ever left the house. She tries to understand why her daughter did what she did. She searches her childhood years. Perhaps, inadvertently, they did treat her differently.

She blames herself. Of course she'd heard about women getting pregnant soon after they adopt. She didn't want it to happen to her. She knew it wouldn't be fair on their new baby. And she never meant it to happen. She thought she was careful. She thought she couldn't have children. It was just one of those things. She'd hoped it would be all right. That the girls would grow close and for a while they did.

But even if they did treat her differently, even if she was affected by the closeness of her sister's birth, it still doesn't explain the actions of the child. After a while she has to give in. Stop thinking about it. She goes back to preparing the tasteless food her daughter has to eat. She goes back to checking to see if she has taken her medication. She goes back to ringing her work, letting them know she's going to need a few more days off.

Her mother pushes and pushes and finally she agrees to go shopping with her. It is her first venture out of the house since her return from the hospital. Her mother says grocery shopping but as soon as they are in the car she starts to talk about clothes, underwear. Her pre hospital clothes no longer fit her. The lack of exercise and special diet has made her blow up to what she thinks is a size 16 balloon. She wears her father's old t-shirts to hide her bulk.

I'm not ready yet.
You don't need to be ready to buy clothes. You never used to.

She doesn't reply and her mother gives in easily. They do the grocery shopping and get back into the car.

She is at a loss for what to do at home so she goes to visit the hospital. It's strange walking back on her own. She goes to find Cherie. Cherie isn't there. She feels more confident in the hospital than she does at home. She likes the feeling. She wanders to the nurse's station to ask where Cherie is. Cherie is out for the day with her mother. She decides to come back tomorrow.

When she gets home her school teacher is at the house. They talk about how much work she has missed. It has been decided, in her absence, that she should stay with her class but it is made clear to her that she is not expected to do well. Next year she will have to repeat. That means she'll be in her sister's year. Maybe in some of the same classes. She says nothing when they tell her this. What can she say? She's glad there will be no expectations. She is also disappointed they didn't think she could catch up.

When she gets to the hospital the next day Cherie is waiting for her.

Heard you came looking for me.
Yeah.
Can't keep you away from the place.
Been up to the roof lately?
Every night.
Why?
Can't sleep.

She wants to ask why? Why can't you sleep? Is it the same reason I can't sleep? And then she thinks about why she can't sleep. Because she is at home. Because she is fat. Because she doesn't want to go to school. Because in some way she knows her life was never meant to be like this and this is not where she should be.

She always looked different from her family. Everyone noticed. You couldn't help but notice. Her family was thin and small, not too short but small. She was large, thick. Her family was light skinned, with fair hair. She had dark hair, she was always heavy coloured. Her mother said there was no such thing as heavy coloured but she knew there was. And she was it. Strangers and friends would comment and even though she wasn't meant to understand she did. It was around that time she started to refuse to be photographed with her family. She preferred to be photographed on her own because that's how she felt when she looked at the photos. Because on her own she didn't look out of place.

The fat girl dreams about life with her natural mother. In her mind they take a thousand photos. The fat girl and her mother. On holiday and at home. Laughing and pulling silly faces. They look exactly the same. Anyone who sees the photos will look at them and know they belong together.

She begins to visit Cherie every day. Her mother disapproves of the amount of time she spends back at the hospital. She visits for this reason as much as she does to see Cherie. They talk now, more than they ever did when she was in the hospital too. She tells Cherie she is adopted. Cherie looks at her, like they all look at her, like she is different. She doesn't care. She tells her baby in the basket on a doorstep story.

Cherie tells her about how many times she's been in there. About the different ways she's tried to kill herself. Cherie is impressed by Anne's method and she is encouraged by this and tells her about her insides. About how she's only got half an intestine left. She hopes Cherie will understand that this explains her appearance. Her fat. They don't talk about why it happened, about why it keeps happening to Cherie. They talk about it like they both know, this is the way the world is.

She's getting her glory back. It's slow and her secret. She hugs it to her self and she feels like she can do anything. She croons over it, tells it how much she has missed it. She starts to smile. Her mother says she's beginning to look like her old self again and puts it down to the time she has been spending with Cherie. Instead of saying she's not ready for school she says she thinks she will start next week. She wants to tell her mother that it is not Cherie, it is her glory that's making her better, making her feel like she's ready to face school again. But instead of speaking she smiles and, for her mother, this is enough.

Her sister is home and she thinks everything will be better now. She makes a special effort to keep out of her way. She wants to ask her questions. She wants to be her friend, her sister. But her sister is too distant, and anyway, her mother said she wasn't allowed to ask questions. So she doesn't speak to her older sister. Not as herself. Sometimes she will say Mum wants to know if ... She is nervous at these times. Before she was in the hospital her sister would yell at her. She doesn't like being yelled at. But now her sister listens and turns away. She rarely answers, sometimes she just says no. Even if it's not a yes or no question. Her sister just says no. Then she has to go back to her mother and shrug her shoulders, which makes her mother sigh.

She has to go back to the hospital for a check up. She doesn't mind. She's there anyway, visiting Cherie. The hospital doctor doesn't approve of the weight she's lost. She tells the doctor it's because of the exercise she's now doing. The doctor frowns at the word exercise too. Not really exercise, she explains, just walking around instead of lying in bed all the time. The doctor remains frowning and questions her on her current diet. She explains again the state her body is now in and reminds her how lucky she is to be alive. She nods through the doctor's words, as if she understands. But she's not listening to the doctor any more, she's listening to her glory.

After her appointment with the doctor she goes to visit Cherie. Cherie is being released the next day. They won't see each other again. They live on opposite sides of the city. They exchange phone numbers anyway and talk as if it's not the last time. She knows she will miss these talks with Cherie. It seems like Cherie is the only friend she has, and then, when she thinks about their friendship, she understands it's not really a friendship at all. It is a coincidence. A chance meeting.

They tell each other they will keep in touch and she believes herself when she says it. She sees herself calling Cherie and arranging to meet in the city. She sees herself sitting next to Cherie watching a movie. She wonders what they will talk about without the security of the hospital around them.

She tells her mother she wants to start doing aerobics. She lies and says the doctor has suggested it would help. Her mother says if she's well enough to do aerobics then she's well enough to go to school. She says, you don't understand and her mother says, then let me, tell me so I do understand and she is silent because she can't think of anything to say.

Her friend from school comes to visit her. Samantha.

They were best friends before the hospital but almost five months away is too long to remain a best friend. Best friends can't be absent, they have to be there, every lunch time, every recess. She knows she has been replaced. She doesn't care. She's not ready to be a best friend again.

Samantha looks at her with a mixture of horror and disgust. She knows why. It's because she is fat. Fatter than she ever was. She is about to explain her new diet, to offer an excuse. But she's not ready to tell Samantha about her insides. Samantha lies and says she looks fine. And then Samantha begins to talk. She talks about school, the other girls, the boys, the teachers. She talks and talks about a world so far away now. A world she doesn't want to be a part of. Samantha asks her when she'll be back and she says soon because she thinks it will make her go away. It does.

The father doesn't see any of the frustration his wife talks about. He sees his daughter, out of that hospital bed and looking better than she has since the accident. They call it an accident, really, he supposes, it should be an incident. But they call it an accident. It makes them believe it won't happen again. He understands his wife's frustration. A woman who worked hard to get back into the work force now having to stay home and babysit a child of 15. He feels their financial concerns. The hospital bills weigh heavily on his mind. Two incomes would relieve that worry.

But he doesn't understand the frustration. She talks about their daughter as if she is manipulative. As if she planned this just to hurt her parents. As if she is enjoying it. He doesn't see any of this when he looks at his daughter. He sees that she is alive and home and he goes back to thinking about work.

Everywhere she turns in the house there is a member of her family. Her bedroom is her only sanctuary. She feels herself boiling inside every time she sees her sister, mother, father. She decides to stay in her room, wait for them to go out so that she can have some time to herself but after a while they knock on her door. To make sure she is all right.

Samantha rings to see if she wants to do anything with her after school hours or on the weekend. She becomes suspicious. She knows Samantha doesn't really want to spend time with her. She's an embarrassment. She knows that from the way Samantha looked at her when she was over the other day. She suspects her mother has set this up. She begins to suspect her mother initiated that first visit. She thinks about agreeing to go out with Samantha, just to make her wish she never agreed to cooperate with her mother. But she can't go out.

She's not ready. Besides, not going will punish her mother.

Why would you want to punish your mother?
She's not my real mother.
She's the only mother you know.
She's always there. She can't leave me alone. Not for a minute. She doesn't trust me.

She has to have these sessions. She didn't want them, but there was no way out. It's the same every time, questions going around in circles. They never get anywhere. She's not even sure where they are meant to go. After a while she stops turning up. They call a few times and then they don't. She suspected they would give up. She knew they didn't really care enough.

Mother and daughter begin to openly argue. She expects her mother to understand. She expects her to understand without explanation. But the mother doesn't understand. The mother is tired of her daughter not being ready. Tired of trying to step carefully around her, trying not to upset her when she doesn't even understand what it is that upsets her. Soon the house becomes unbearable for both of them. The daughter is forced to return to school and the mother returns to work.

When the younger sister sees the older sister walking down the school corridor it is a shock but it is good. It's the way things should be. She wants to hug her and tell her how happy she is to see her there. She wants to tell her how much better it will make things now she is out of the house, away from the arguing. But she doesn't do either of these things. Instead she tries to catch her eye. To give her an encouraging smile but the older sister purposely looks away.

I hear my parents talking through the wall.

I just don't know what to do.

My mother.

I don't think there's anything we can do.

My father.

At least she's gone back to school.
It's still not right. Something's not right.

I recall how my mother likes everything on the mantlepiece to be a certain way and how she'll move things back without thinking if they happen to change position.

We have to expect that it takes time.

I recall how my father will unknowingly, unthinkingly, move objects on the mantlepiece.

She seems much better to me.

When she goes back to school it's like walking into a nightmare. It's not the work load. She has been excused of any responsibility as far as school work. All she has to do is turn up. To try. That makes it harder. Now she's even more different from everyone else. Now everyone else knows how different from them she is. She tries to avoid the other students but they all want to talk to her. They want to know where she's been, how she got out of so much school work. They want to know her illness, want her to describe in full detail her hospital experience. She doesn't know how to answer their questions. Instead she evades their questions and tries to avoid the people who ask them. She keeps her head down and tries to remember that all she has to do is to be there.

She skips a few days of school. Convinces her mother that she needs the time to herself. She is surprised that her mother agrees. She begins to think her mother has given up fighting her and sees this as a good sign. She doesn't do anything on these days off. She enjoys her solitude. She throws away the lunches her mother carefully prepares and exercises in a way her doctor says she shouldn't and her glory says she must. She looks at her body in the mirror and even though it still disgusts her she begins to feel like she can control it.

She returns to school again. She returns to the same feeling of being left behind, to the same, insistent questions. But this time she has the answers prepared. She takes on the appearance of enjoying herself. She gives flippant answers to the questions they ask, laughs and jokes about her time away. They begin to accept her answers or understand that she doesn't want to talk about it and she begins to hope that soon they will stop asking.

Her sister begins to look happy. She watches her and every now and then she sees it. Her sister catches her looking and before she can turn away, her sister smiles. Sister to sister, the elder smiles. The younger sister tries to think of the last time her sister smiled at her but soon gets defeated. She imagines how everything could change. She sees her sister walking with her to school. Maybe next year they'll be in some of the same classes. They could sit next to each other. She sees them going to movies together, friends as well as sisters. Her sister would tell her secrets and she would hold on to them, precious secrets, she'd never tell anyone, because that's what sisters are for.

When they were young they used to play together. She thinks she remembers playing with her sister but the memories are enhanced by the photographs. She asks her mother and her mother says they were so close in age that it was natural they played together. She doesn't remember when it stopped or why. Her mother can't explain it. But she remembers that it stopped. It stopped and then it just got worse until she started to become treated like an enemy.

Samantha is pleased to see her back to her old self. She cringes at the expression. Her old self got caught, got caught in the worst possible way. She can't afford to let her new self be seen like that. She doesn't tell her friend this. Doesn't correct her assumption like she wants to. Doesn't say 'I'm new now, this is my new self, and it's so much better', because she's not sure it is and because her friend wouldn't understand. Instead she accepts the friendship and enjoys the familiarity it offers.

Samantha invites her to a party. She says yes. Her parents are surprised and too pleased for her to feel comfortable about it. When the night arrives she doesn't want to go. Her glory forces her to dress, to walk out of her room. Her parents look nervous as she leaves and she tries not to let them see the fear in her eyes. Her friend promises to take care of her and she begins to feel like a child, leaving the house unprotected for the very first time.

When they get to the party it's a quiet affair. They sit together in a corner and giggle. They talk about all the people they can see, all the people they know at school. They talk like they used to talk. They don't talk about the hospital, about her, how she's feeling and if she's okay. They talk outside themselves and they are safe, together at the party. She begins to relax, the hospital is over now, she is back. And she has her glory.

The fat girl dreams she is walking down the street. A busy city street. She's swinging her arms in a carefree way. The fat girl dreams it's a warm summer day. She's walking down the street, swinging her arms but not sweating. She feels warm and free. She catches sight of herself in a shop front window. Her hair is long, down to the middle of her back, and it falls like it has just been brushed. The fat girl holds her breath as she looks down her body. Size 8, maybe even smaller. She becomes conscious that she is staring at herself in the mirror. She begins to walk again. Now she can feel people looking at her. Men and women. They're staring because she's thin. Because she's swinging her arms in such a carefree manner. The fat girl dreams she's about to go shopping. She's going to try everything on, safe in the knowledge that if it doesn't look good it's because it doesn't suit her, not because she's fat.

She quickly slips back into her old routine. She and Samantha spend their Saturdays in the city. They try on clothes and hang out, sipping diet drinks, which are on her list of things she should not consume.

They look at boys from other schools, boys who don't go to school, men. Samantha has become interested in older men. She fakes an interest similar to her friend's but she's not interested in the men they see. They all look strange and unfamiliar. They too would ask her questions about the hospital, about her list. They would look at her and see her as different.

One Saturday she sees Cherie. She knows her immediately even though she's had her hair cut. She panics. It's different now, she's different now, and she's with her school friend. She remembers the roof, the hospital, she and Cherie talking in the ward, how she almost told her what she doesn't even know. She doesn't know what to do. All the time she is thinking, worrying, Cherie is moving closer and closer. She sees that Cherie is with her own friends. Maybe she won't want to talk to her. Maybe she'll just walk by and pretend they never saw each other, they never knew each other, they were never in the hospital. Cherie sees her. Their eyes lock in recognition. She says something to the girls she is with and moves away from them. She's walking towards her now. This is her chance to move away from Samantha, so that she can talk to her alone. She stays where she is. She's afraid to walk, afraid her legs will shake. Besides, she looks thinner sitting down.

Hi.

Hi.

Out in the real world now hey?

Yeah. You too.

Yeah.

You still at school?

Yeah. You?

Yeah, but I'm thinking of quitting.

Why?

She shrugs.

Hate it. You should give me a call sometime.

Yeah, okay.

She doesn't say that she has. She wants to say, I did call, you weren't home. I really wanted to talk to you but you weren't home. She doesn't say that. That would sound weird.

Well see you.

Yeah see you.

Call.

Okay.

Samantha is curious about Cherie. She is surprised that she hasn't been mentioned before. She tries to answer her friend's questions as best she can. She really doesn't know what to say.

We were in the same ward.

Why was she there?

One night she woke me up and took me on to the roof. We drank scotch and looked at the stars.

What did it taste like?

What?

The scotch.

I don't know. Scotch.

Samantha falls silent. She can see she has other questions she wants to ask. But she doesn't want to talk about the hospital with Samantha. She knew what she said would shut her up. She knew she wouldn't know how to react because she's never sat on a roof and drunk scotch and looked at the stars. Because she'd never want to.

It gets harder and harder to hide her glory. Her mother starts to make her special tasteless food in larger and larger portions. Her mother studies her body carefully under the oversized clothes she wears and suggests she looks thin. She doesn't say it like it's a compliment. The larger portions are harder to dispose of, harder to throw up afterwards. She sees that again her mother is trying to destroy her glory. The only thing she has that is really hers, her mother wants to take away. But she won't let her. She just has to find a way around her. It isn't easy, her mother is there all the time. Always watching her, always asking questions. She tries to say the right thing in the hope that saying the right thing will make her stop watching. Stop cooking. There doesn't seem to be a right thing to say.

School no longer requires any effort on her part. As the year draws to its end and everyone around her is working hard and worrying about passing maths, she is drawing pictures in her notebook and thinking about her glory. It has been decided that it would be useless for her to try and sit any of the tests and she doesn't see the point in trying to learn anything she will only have to repeat in the next year and will probably forget over the holidays anyway. So she draws pictures in her notebook and looks out the window. She wonders what she'll do with her life. She doesn't want to think about next year. About the years she has left at the school and in her parents' house. She wants to think about after school, when she's working and living on her own.

She looks around the classroom and wonders what they'll be doing when she's an independent woman. Her eyes rest on the boy sitting in the next row, one seat further to the front. He's drawing too. She tries to see what he's drawing but the angle is wrong. He turns around, catching her stare. She's been caught. It's too late to look away. She smiles. Her glory makes her do it. She sits there and smiles at the boy in her maths class who doesn't care about the upcoming tests either. She is embarrassed by her smile but it's too late now. He smiles back. Her glory was right to start the smile.

She decides to call Cherie. She waits near the phone, wishing the rest of her family would leave the house. She's memorised the number. Every time she moves towards the phone her father will come into the room, or her sister, or her mother. Or she'll hear them moving nearby, and she knows they'll be able to hear her if she rings. She can't do it if she knows people are listening. She waits. Her father walks into the room with the newspaper. He settles himself into a chair. She decides to call from the phone box down the road.

Cherie's mother answers the phone.

Uh, hello, could I speak to Cherie please?

She hears the phone drop and her mother yell.

Cherie!
What?!
Phone! Don't talk too long I'm waiting for a call.
Hello?

She nearly hangs up.

Hello, Cherie?

Yeah, who's this?

It's Anne.

How're you?

Okay. You?

Sick of school. I'm going to drop out.

Really?

Yeah. Waste of time.

I wish I could. What will you do?

I don't know. Get a job. Where are you?

Phone box, down the road. No privacy at my house.

Yeah. Listen I can't talk long.

Oh. Well I just called to see how you're doing.

Okay. Well I'll talk to you again then.

Okay.

Maybe we can do something sometime.

Okay.

See you.

Bye.

When she hangs up the phone she feels disappointed. She doesn't know what she expected from
the phone call. Maybe someone who would understand her. A friend who knew why she was in the
hospital and didn't care, because she was there too.
Cherie didn't sound like a friend. Just someone she

51

met once. Lucky though, to be able to leave school like that.

She thought everything would be all right when her daughter went back to school. She seems happier, more at ease with herself. She even smiles now, although a lot of the time it's fake. At least she's trying. She knows it's hard for her daughter at school, hard for her to go there each day knowing she'll just have to do it again next year. Some days her daughter comes home, tired and defeated and the mother wants to cry. Wants to hold her, take the world away from her and give her what she wants. What would make her happy. Instead she asks her questions about her day and when her daughter says she hates it, that there's no point going, her response comes out sharper than she wants. It's her fault she ended up in hospital, she did it to herself. Now she just has to get through the year. And the year after that. There's nothing else that can be done. She just has to keep going. Her daughter looks like at any moment she'll stop. And the mother wants to correct herself. Let the daughter know she'll help, if the daughter would let her, would tell her how, she would help.

But the daughter never tells. Never tells her anything. And when she speaks to her daughter it's the anger and her frustration that come out. It's her fear and her confusion that makes her snap and then turn away so she doesn't have to watch her daughter leave.

She watches him now. It makes her look forward to maths. She wants to know why he doesn't care about school work. She knows his name. Daniel. He doesn't seem to have any friends at the school. No one she knows anyway. He's new. Only arrived in the area this year. She doesn't know where he came from. She'd like to ask. Like to know more about him. But for the moment she's happy just watching him in her maths class. She's happy knowing there's someone else, kind of like her.

When he speaks to her she feels her glory grow. It glows inside of her, radiates in her eyes, her smile. He speaks to her after school, catches her as she is about to walk home. He never asked her about the hospital, about why she was away. He doesn't now. He doesn't even talk about school work the way the other kids do. He talks about the world, about life. He talks about things she never thought to talk about. And then he is gone, leaving her with her glory glowing.

When she tells Samantha, she says he's not cool. Not like them. She doesn't care, she likes him she says and her friend looks at her, silent and disapproving. She still doesn't care. She has her glory, getting bigger all the time.

Two

I'm standing on a cliff. Below me I can see the ocean. It's so far away it looks harmless as it falls on the rocks.

Behind me are my parents and younger sister. They're sitting on a blanket, eating.

But I am standing. Standing on the edge of a cliff.

I turn and walk back to where my family are sitting. I sit with them and take a bread roll. My mother says something but I can't understand what it is. The wind has taken her words. It blows them down the cliff. I get up to follow them and imagine myself tumbling down the cliff after my mother's words. Somehow I think it won't hurt. I want to follow those words and understand their meaning but by the time I reach the cliff edge they have gone.

I stand looking for the words. I throw my bread roll after them. I become angry that I can't see them, that she didn't give me the chance to see them.

I walk back towards my family but I don't sit down. Instead I pass where they are sitting. I start to run, through the car park and back onto the road. I run away from my family and away from my mother's words.

I run like I will never stop.

The fat girl has always had to try hard. She always has to be better. Because no one wants the fat girl. No one likes fat people. All her life the fat girl has had to try to be better than she is. Better than the people around her. Otherwise they'll give her away, pass her on to someone else. People don't like to be around fat. It's like a disease. They think they'll catch it.

She's working. It took a few days to get the hang of it but now she pushes the groceries over the scanner without even thinking. She picks up a tub of ice-cream. Icecream is hard because it gets ice on the barcode. Sometimes you have to scrape it off with your fingernail. This one goes through on the third try. She looks up at the customer. An older guy. Maybe in his thirties. She wonders if he's looking at her body in the uniform. She asked for a bigger size but they gave her this one. It's too tight. Even her mother says it's too tight.

The customer fumbles around for money and hands it to her. His hand is warm and damp. Not like Daniel's hands. Daniel's hands are cool and dry. She looks at her next customer. An older woman whose trolley is heaped full of this week's specials. She looks at the clock. It's still two hours before her lunch break and then another four before she finishes.

She's already tired but she doesn't care. She's working.

School was over for her. She was still required to attend but there was nothing for her there. She started to bring in magazines. The teacher suggested she read the novels on the next year's syllabus but she brought in magazines. The teacher didn't argue. There was nothing she could say anyway. Everyone told her when she came back, all she had to do was turn up.

Samantha had no time to talk to her. She was busy swapping notes with other people and worrying about the end of year tests. In the time they did spend together they didn't have much to say. It was like she was being left behind. Everyone was going somewhere and she wasn't invited. She said this to Samantha but Samantha denied it. Said she was being dramatic and it wouldn't change anything. But it already had.

She tried to imagine the following year and her life after that. She couldn't see herself finishing high school. She had no desire to go to university, no great dream of being a lawyer or archaeologist. She started to find the thought of more school years unbearable. She began to daydream about a job. She wasn't sure what sort of job she could get at the time. She saw herself working in a café, not serving food, making coffee. She would make coffee all day until the smell was in her hair and on her skin. She would meet interesting people in the café. Perhaps one day she would have one of her own. Of course she doesn't know how to make coffee but she could learn. It couldn't be that hard.

She started to look in the employment pages. She even went into a few cafés to ask for work. That's when she found out what sort of work she could get. Cafés wouldn't employ someone as young as her, offices wouldn't employ someone who hadn't completed year 10. There was only one job she could get and that was a supermarket job. Cherie told her. She was working in her local supermarket. She said it wasn't so bad. She liked stacking shelves and sometimes cute guys came in.

She wanted to work in Cherie's supermarket but to get there would take an hour, almost two, and they wouldn't hire someone who lived so far away. So she went to one closer. They asked her a lot of questions and got her to fill in a form. She lied about her age. Cherie said you have to and anyway, they don't care.

They didn't call her straight away. She thought they weren't going to and started to think about another supermarket or perhaps a cleaning job. But then they called. It was getting close to Christmas and they needed extra staff. If she worked well they would talk after the New Year about keeping her on. The wage was minimal but she didn't care. It meant she wouldn't have to go back to school, repeat her year and risk being in classes with her sister.

When she is with Daniel the fat girl whispers in her ear.

Don't sit like that, it makes you look fat. Sit the other way. The way you practised.
Don't smile like that.
Your hair's falling out of shape.
Your breath is bad, don't breathe in his direction.
Don't say that. That's a stupid thing to say. That's what a fat person would say.

She shuts her mouth, crosses her legs and opens her eyes wide, the way she practised, to make her look more interested. She can't ignore the fat girl.

It's Friday. Two hours before she finishes work. She'll sign off her time sheet tonight and then next week she'll get paid. Her second pay. She hasn't spent much of the first yet. She's saving it for something she really wants. After work she'll go home and shower and then she'll meet Daniel at their spot, half a block down from the bus stop. He said it was half way between their houses but she knows it's closer to hers. It makes her smile to think that he planned it like that. So she wouldn't have to walk so far.

Maybe they'll see a movie or just sit in some fast food place and talk. She prefers to see movies, where they sit in the dark. In the beginning they sit close, so close they're almost touching, but they aren't. By the end of the movie they are. Shoulders and arms touching. His hand holding hers. Her hand holding his. She likes to hold his hand.

After the movie or when it's time for her to go home, he'll walk with her, still holding her hand. Before they get to her house he'll kiss her. She always imagines it will be long and passionate. Really it's awkward and a bit wet. She doesn't care. She'll get shy and say her parents are waiting and then run into the house. He'll say 'I'll call you' and she knows he will. She'll fall asleep thinking of their night and before the fat girl can tell her everything she did wrong, in that moment when she keeps the fat girl quiet, she'll smile.

She didn't tell her parents about her plan. She didn't tell them she was looking for a job. Even when they called and said she got the job she still didn't tell them. She wanted to. She practised in her head. She asked Cherie and Cherie gave her a few suggestions. Cherie's mother was glad she was working. Cherie paid board and her mother said she was a big help.

So that was what she said.

I can help with the hospital bills.

She knew her parents were still paying them.

Or I could pay board.
We don't want your money. We want you to go to school.
I'm sick of going to school.
You're throwing your life away.

They were right but she didn't tell them. She didn't want her life. No one wanted her life. So she was throwing it away. She was making a new life. Maybe no one would want that one either. At least she was trying. She didn't understand why her parents couldn't see that she was trying.

When the mother looked at her daughter, her elder child, leaving for school every morning, she felt strong. She saw her daughter as strong. They had faced a terrible illness and they had won. The mother tries not to think about what it would have been like if her daughter had died. It makes her cry.

But watching her leave for school every morning made

her feel strong. And now that wasn't going to happen any more. It made her feel weak. Her daughter has taken her strength away again. She wonders how it happens. If she lets it happen. They decide not to argue with her. She has already said yes to the job. She hopes it will only last until Christmas and then she'll go back to school.

The family settled quickly into the routine of the summer. Her parents would go to work every morning, like they always did. She would go to work too, carrying the lunch prepared carefully by her mother. Her younger sister would stay at home. She was enjoying her holidays even though she said she was bored. At night they would gather for the evening meal. Sometimes her sister prepared it for them. They would all talk or complain about their day and then they would separate into their own sections of the house. Her mother still worried that she wasn't eating enough or that work was too much of a strain on her. She still hated the idea of her daughter working but there were no arguments, no more discussions about whether or not she would continue to work after the summer. It felt like they had reached a kind of peace.

She walks to meet Daniel at their spot. He's there waiting when she arrives. He's always there waiting. She approaches him with her heart pounding. She is always nervous at first. She makes an effort not to let it show. Daniel never says anything so she thinks she hides it well.

As they wait for the bus to take them into the city they think of things to say. Daniel is looking for a job too. She thought he could work in the super-market with her. Maybe in the fruit and vegetable section. But Daniel doesn't want to work in a super-market. He refuses to wear a uniform. His parents don't mind if he gets a job. Daniel has never been very good at school. It's only her parents who think you should finish school.

When they get to the city they choose a fast food place and take a seat. Once they went to a café but the prices were too expensive for them. She drinks coffee as she watches Daniel eat a burger and fries. She used to drink something diet but ever since she's been working she drinks coffee. It makes her feel older.

When he spoke to her after school her glory filled her. She became the girl in her head not the girl in the mirror. When he asked her to go out with him her glory grew even bigger. She didn't know it could. It stayed that big until he left her alone and then it abandoned her as she thought about asking her parents and what she would wear.

She didn't ask her parents until her date was only

a few hours away. She thought about it. All week she thought about it but the words never left her mouth. Now they had to. She considered lying but she hadn't been spending time with any of her old friends. Her parents knew this. So she told them. They said no.

I am going. You can't stop me.
If you leave this house …

My mother.

You can't stop me.
Try me.

I've never seen my mother this mad.

I just want to be like the other kids.
You're not going out with a boy we haven't even met.

My father.

Do your friend's parents let them do that?
Yes.

I lie.

Well not you.

They know.

Now get ready for dinner.
I'm not hungry.

The sister is upset by the argument. She is upset by her sister looking like she's going to cry and slamming her bedroom door. She is upset by her parents not speaking through dinner, excluding her from their thoughts. The sister wants to help. She wants to tell them that all the girls her sister's age have boyfriends. She wants to go to her sister and tell her it's all right. She doesn't need a boyfriend. But she knows she won't do either of these things, so she eats her dinner silently and tries not to look at her parents.

Her sister stays in her room all night. Even when she taps nervously on the door there's no reply. Later the sister asks quietly through the door if there is anything she can do, anything she wants. There is no answer. The sister takes all her courage and uses it to open the door. The room is empty. She closes the door and tells her parents her sister has fallen asleep.

By the end of their date she is feeling bad. They have spent the night wandering around the city. They looked at seeing a movie but there was nothing they wanted to see. As they wandered aimlessly through the city they saw some other people they knew from school. Everyone acted like strangers and the sighting left her with a bad feeling. She was feeling good about her job and about Daniel but after seeing those people, who were as happy to ignore her, as she was to ignore them, she feels bad.

She wonders what they think of seeing her with Daniel. Whether they're laughing at her. She wonders if they know she is working in a supermarket. If they laugh about that too. She wants to go home, go to sleep, forget about her night but she can't. She fought hard to stay out until 11pm so now she just has to wait out her time. She worries because her glory has gone home without her.

She only left the house one other time, without her parents knowing, before she was caught. With the close watch they keep on her she wonders how she got away with it those first two times. When they catch her they are angry. She can see the anger on their faces and she can see them both trying to control it.

It was a Friday night. Their elder daughter went to bed early saying she was tired. She often went to bed before them and they thought nothing of it. Later, when the mother rose to say she was going to check on her, the younger daughter jumped to her feet.

I'll go.

She looked nervous. The mother refused her offer and went herself. This is when she found the room empty. The mother was furious. After all the pain and worry and expense this daughter had put them through. After everything that had happened she was still deceiving them. And the younger daughter knew.

The mother went back to the lounge room and studied her daughter waiting guiltily.

Where is she?
I don't know.

And the younger sister didn't. She told them everything she suspected. She didn't tell them it had happened before.

The parents sat together in the lounge room long after the younger daughter had gone to bed. They didn't speak much. For a while they had the television on but it had become a distraction to their own private thoughts and had been turned off.

When she arrived home after her second date with Daniel and saw the lights still on she knew she had been discovered. She didn't care. She wanted them to know. When she walked through the door they were there waiting for her. They took her to the lounge room and they sat down and they talked. They know she hates to talk but they persisted until they found out what they needed to know. Then they insisted on meeting Daniel and made her promise not to lie to them again. But she'd been lying every day. How could she not?

On Monday she doesn't feel like going to work. She can't stay at home because her mother would worry and she would be with her sister all day. She dresses for work as if it were any other work day. She tries to avoid looking in the mirror as she does every day but can't. Not today. She stares at her reflection, hating the sight of her body in the too tight dress. She pulls herself away and goes to eat the breakfast her mother has prepared. The breakfast her mother always prepares. She leaves for work like she always does but stops at the phone box to call work and tell them she is sick. She thinks about calling Daniel but decides against it. He'd only make her feel worse.

She walks to a café nearby and orders a coffee. While she is waiting for her coffee she finds a copy of the weekend paper. She starts to flick through the real estate pages and fantasises about owning her own house.

When she gets home that night she is quiet. She's been thinking all day. She hasn't made any resolutions about her life, she has just been thinking. Thinking about what she could make her life to be. What she would want her life to be if she were thin and if she had lots of money. She hasn't found any answers but she knows the house would be part of it. Her own house where she would live alone. It would be two levels, with thick carpet in some rooms and cool tiles in others.

Her family doesn't comment on her mood at dinner. It's not unusual for her to be silent. After dinner she goes straight to her room so she can think about where the bathroom would be.

She spends the rest of the week working. It's busy as people start to prepare for Christmas. She likes it when it's busy because the time flies by. Her feet get tired from standing all day but she just tells them to get used to it. This is what she plans to do next year. She won't let her body stop her.

The customers' shopping trolleys get bigger and bigger as they contemplate that time when the supermarket will be closed for a few days. She works longer hours as the demand grows greater and, as she scans can after can after frozen peas, she calculates in her head how much she is earning and wonders when it will be enough to buy her house.

When they were at school Daniel didn't have any friends. That's why it was so good for her glory when he spoke to her. He had chosen to be alone and then he chose to be with her. Samantha said he was weird but she didn't care. He wasn't ugly, he just preferred to be on his own. And he had picked her. Out of all the girls in her class, in the school, he had chosen to speak to her.

Samantha said not having any friends was a bad sign, she said it meant he was more than weird. But still she didn't care. She thought maybe he had other friends outside of school. Or maybe he just didn't like to be around people. She understood that. But now, as their times together become more and more boring, she begins to rethink her attitude about his lack of friends. Her boredom is killing her glory just when she thought it had grown hard and stable and no one could take it away.

The girls are bitching in the tearoom. She is sitting with them as they smoke their cigarettes and drink their coffee with milk and sugar. They talk about the girls who aren't in the room and the managers who make them miserable. They talk about the men who work there, who's married, who isn't. Who's sexy, who isn't. Only two of these women are married, they join the conversation but smile at each other as if they know a secret.

She doesn't have anything to say. They tease her about being so quiet and demand to know if she has a boyfriend. She thinks about Daniel. She doesn't want to tell these women about him so she shakes her head. They laugh at her because she had to think about it and accuse her of lying. She looks at her watch, there's still five minutes left. She smiles at them again and pretends her break is over as she quickly leaves the room.

She tries not to ask every day.

How was work?
Fine.
How are you feeling?
Fine.
Did you eat your lunch?

Silent stare.

Well?
I'm going to take a shower.

She never eats her lunch. At work she drinks a cup of coffee in her lunch break or takes a walk around the other shops near the supermarket. Sometimes she'll eat an apple. Lots of girls at work will just have a coffee or cigarette. No one asks her questions at work when they see that she is not eating because it's not unusual there.

But her mother asks her every day. If she says yes her mother will ask her what she had. Then she has to try to remember what her mother made. Every day she carries the package her mother prepares. It sits on her lap on the bus. As soon as she gets off the bus she throws it in the bin. She'd throw it away before the bus ride but she thought her mother might check the bin. So she looks at it once to see what's there and then she throws it away. She knows if she ate it, it would taste bad and make her fatter. She tries to avoid her mother's questions about lunch. Once she told her she had gone to a lunch bar with some of the girls and eaten there. Her mother just sighed that time as she imagined her daughter eating foods she knows her body can't handle.

She goes to the supermarket where her sister works. She says they have run out of rice and need it for dinner that night. She waits behind a mother of four and a man who is making the most of a sale on laundry powder and icecream so she can go through her sister's checkout. The elder sister points out that another line would have been faster but the sister shrugs. She's not in a hurry.

Really she wants to see where her sister works. She wants to know what she looks like behind the till. Her sister is suspicious. She wants to know if it was the mother who sent her. The younger sister hadn't expected this and her surprise makes her look innocent. She leaves the super-market quickly. She didn't think her sister would stop work and talk to her but she had hoped ... She doesn't know what she hoped. Something slower and more friendly. Something that would show her that her sister really did like her.

She's tired of spending a weekend night with Daniel. She's tired trying to fill the time until 11pm. When he rings on Wednesday night to arrange their date for the weekend she agrees. As she says yes and they make their plans, she tells herself it will be the last time. He's killing her glory. She imagines herself telling him this.

I'm sorry but I can't see you anymore. You're killing my glory.

Would he ask her to explain? Would he beg her to change her mind? That would make her glory grow again. If he begged her not to break up with him. If he got so upset he nearly cried. But she knows it wouldn't last. Her glory needs something else now. Its own house, or maybe someone new. She hangs up the phone after agreeing to meet Daniel at the usual place, to do the usual things and tells herself again it will be the last time.

When she arrives at work on Thursday morning there's a new girl working. The new girl isn't shy like she was on her first day. The supervisor introduces them.

Anne, this is Amanda. She'll be replacing Margaret.

Amanda extends her hand.

Mandy.

She shakes Mandy's hand and smiles.

Hi.
Anne, I thought you could show her where the tearoom and toilet is.
Okay.

Mandy's arrival means two things. If they are replacing Margaret, an older woman who left because her husband got a better job, then they still need her. And if they still need her that means Mandy is now the new girl, so if anyone is going to be fired after the Christmas and New Year rush then it will be Mandy, not her. Unless Mandy turns out to be better than she is, or they like her more. But that didn't really happen here. They didn't care enough. So long as you turned up and did your hours, the sackings would start with the newest employee and work their way back.

Samantha rings.

I haven't heard from you in a while.
No.

She hasn't even thought about her friend or school. She thought it was all over.

So … what have you been up to?

I've been really busy.

I heard you were working.

Yeah.

Samantha doesn't ask about Daniel. If she knows that she's working then she knows she's still going out with Daniel. She wants to tell her they're breaking up. She wants to tell her to go away. She wants to live in a place that's so big no one knows if you're working or going out with Daniel. Samantha talks about herself, about what she's been doing like Samantha always does. She stays silent.

Well, I should probably get going. We should get together some time.

Okay. Thanks for calling.

After she hangs up, she thinks about the phone call. She thinks about the things she could have said. She thinks about her friend, reporting back to the other girls from school. They would laugh at the idea of her working in a supermarket. They would laugh at the thought of her in a uniform. She should have told her. Told her how great it is. How with the money she can do anything she wants, get a place of her own or go travelling. She should have told her about the cute fruit and veg guy and the new girl Mandy who seems pretty cool.

On Friday she has the same lunch break as Mandy. They sit across the table from one another. She eats an apple. Mandy eats a ham and salad roll. Afterwards she has a cigarette and coffee with milk. She wants to talk to Mandy. Wants to be her friend. Mandy is two years older than her. She looks like she's been sitting in the tearoom all her life and could look like that anywhere. She still feels like a stranger in the tearoom.

Mandy asks her about the supervisors, the other women and the cute fruit and veg guy. She tells her what she knows. This supervisor is a bitch, this one is okay and will let you stack shelves if you don't feel like being on the till. She tells her which of the women are married, divorced or in between. Who has kids, who wants kids, and about the younger ones, who's still going to school and who's looking for a better job in a dress shop. She doesn't know much about the fruit and veg guy. She admits he's cute but has no more information to offer. Mandy asks what she is doing on the weekend. She says she's breaking up with her boyfriend. She finds this an impressive thing to say, so she elaborates. She's tired of him, he used to be fun but now he's dull, so she's going to dump him. Mandy is suitably impressed. She says when Anne's single they should go out some time. She says, *yeah. That would be cool.*

And inside her glory begins to shine because she is making a new friend.

He has forgotten the pain and anxiety of the hospital. Forgotten the long hours of worry and the tension that remained in the back of his neck every night as he tried to get to sleep. He has forgotten how frail his daughter looked, how delicate her life became. His memory of the hospital is tied up in the bills they still have to pay. He concentrates every month on making that total lower. He no longer sees his daughter in the number. It's just a number now. A number he has to work at to make zero. But when he looks at his elder daughter, he sees her as cured. A little unhappy maybe, making choices he would rather she didn't make, but cured.

Every time she looks at her elder daughter the hospital comes back into her mind and she searches her daughter's face for a sign she may be returning. She can't tell if she's better or worse. She cannot claim to understand more than her husband but she can't forget. Can't forget it was a mind illness and that it could return. She tries not to push. She tries not to ask every day but sometimes she has to ask, sometimes she can't find enough in her daughter's purposely expressionless face to satisfy her anxiety and she has to ask, how are you? She says it lightly, she remembers to ask her younger daughter the same question. How are you? The older daughter responds fine, always fine. But she can tell by the way she says fine. She can tell something's still not right.

She resents him for being able to forget so easily. She tells him this. He says what more is there for him to do. She has no answer. She tries to tell him how she feels and he says what can I do to help, and she doesn't know. She wants him to take some of her pain, to share her burden, but he did that before and he doesn't feel the pain any more. So she is left alone. He says let it go, leave her be for a while, but she can't.

She arrives late to their meeting spot on Friday night. She wants to miss the bus into the city. She's been thinking about what to say but she hasn't worked it out yet. She wants to tell him about her glory. She wants to say, *you're killing my glory. I can't spend any more boring Friday nights with you because I'll lose my glory.* She knows she can't say this. Instead she apologises for being late. Daniel says it doesn't matter but she can tell he's annoyed about missing the bus. She takes a breath, finds her glory and tells him she doesn't want to see him any more. She adds the bit about still being friends. She knows that's what you're meant to do. Daniel looks surprised and then relieved. She is annoyed by his look of relief. She was hoping he would be upset but cool enough not to make a scene. They don't say much. Daniel kisses her like a friend, or how she imagines a friend would kiss and they go their separate ways. She knows she is going to go to her room and cry but she doesn't know why.

Her sister cries on the other side of the wall and the younger sister wonders how many times she's heard it before. She lies there listening until she stops hearing and becomes interested in other things. It's not until a few hours later, when she goes to bed, that she realises the crying has stopped. As she falls asleep she thinks about her sister. She has thought so much about her since those months in hospital. The mystery she is. Her sister is a favourite and constant conversation among her school friends. They can't work her out. They are confused by why she seems so unhappy. She doesn't have to go to school.

On Monday she arrives at work a few minutes early. Mandy is in the tearoom having her before work cigarette and coffee. She's keen to know how the break up went. Did she have the nerve to do it? She is relieved she doesn't have to lie. She doesn't tell her about the relieved look on Daniel's face. Instead she tells her he was disappointed but took it quite well and they agreed to be friends. Mandy nods approvingly. She quickly states she has no intention of keeping in touch but she felt it was the right thing to say. Mandy butts out her cigarette and says that now she's free they can party together. She smiles at Mandy and inside she begins her feel her glory grow.

She spends her day stocking shelves and scanning food. She begins to notice how much meat people buy. She never thought before about how much meat people seem to need, how much they must eat. She thinks maybe it's just Christmas because every trolley that comes her way is full of meat and she didn't notice it so much before, when she first started. The meat bleeds onto the checkout and she has to keep getting out a cloth to wipe it down. Sometimes it drips on her as she puts it into the plastic bags before handing it to the customers. She begins to find it disturbing and looks forward to her break when she can go and wash her hands.

On her way home she plans a way to avoid the evening meal. She knows her plan will make her mother anxious but it has to be done. She will endure her mother's nagging if it means she'll have her glory firmly in hand when she goes out with Mandy. When she gets home she announces she's not feeling well and goes straight to bed. Her mother follows her to her room, as she has imagined she would.

What's wrong? Do you feel sick?
A little.

Headache?

Just kind of tired.

You can't go to sleep without eating.

I'll just lie down before dinner.

She knows if she is asleep when it comes time for dinner her mother won't wake her. Instead she'll hope that she wakes up herself and comes into the kitchen to ask for some food. They both know this won't happen.

The sister is excited to be sitting next to her elder sister on the bus. It was her mother's suggestion they catch the bus together. Her mother's suggestion she spend her day with her friend. Her friend who just happens to live on the same bus route as her sister's supermarket. She doesn't even really want to spend her day with her friend. She's quite happy spending her days at home. But that doesn't matter now. Now that she's sitting on the bus with her sister.

She wants to tell her, wants to say, you remember when you first went out with Daniel? And then before her sister could reply she'd say, I knew you were gone, I went into your room and you weren't there so I lied for you. She imagines this will start a conversation full of secrets and things she's never understood before.

But they sit silently next to each other on the bus. Her

sister doesn't speak. She opens her mouth, heart pounding only suddenly they are at her sister's stop and her sister's leaving, going to her job, saying goodbye and the younger sister is left with her mouth open, words forming, as the elder sister walks away.

She doesn't notice her sister sitting next to her on the bus. She's thinking about going out with Mandy. How she has to get ready. How she has to get thin. She can't go straight to bed every night. Her mother will worry too much. She'll say that she is sick again and make her go back to the hospital and she can't go back to the hospital. Not now. They'll take her glory away.

Mandy winks at her across the checkouts. She mouths the words 'see you at lunch' and she smiles and nods in return. She feels her glory pounding inside her. This is the invitation. She knows she is right. This is the invitation.

It's to a party. Saturday night. A friend of a friend but Mandy says it will be cool. She believes her because she's older, because she hangs out with people who are even older, and because of the way she says it. She says it slowly and confidently. Like she's looked at the sky and told her it's blue. She knows, the party will be cool. They agree to make a plan on Friday and then Mandy goes back to her checkout. She still has another fifteen minutes left of her lunch break so she sits and imagines what the party will be like and worries because there's not enough time to get thin.

She doesn't like to throw up. She tries not to do it. It's bad for her glory. But her glory has no choice. She has to be thin before the weekend. Before she meets Mandy's friends. There's nothing else she can do.

And then she did something she thought she'd never do. She questioned her younger child about her elder. Pushing one against the other. She knows something isn't right. She knows their relationship is hard enough without her making it worse. But she has justified her actions to herself. Her elder daughter will never tell her if something's wrong. And she knows something's wrong. She wants to stop it early. More than anything else she doesn't want to go through another illness. So she questions her younger daughter, knowing it will push them further apart, wondering if it will push them together, against her.

I want you to tell me what's going on with your sister.

How should I know?

You mean you don't?

She hardly knows I exist.

You'd tell me if anything was wrong wouldn't you?

86

She watches her daughter squirm.

You want her to get sick again?

She knows it's a threat.

You would tell me wouldn't you? If anything was seriously wrong?

And the younger daughter is forced to say yes.

She's fighting now. Fighting for her glory. She goes to work fighting. Comes home fighting. At work it's easy. She lets her glory run free. She feels strong at work, fighting side by side with her glory. At home it gets harder. She knows her family would take her glory away if they knew of its existence. She knows they would try to kill it if they knew it was fighting. So she has to be careful. She has to make sure the fighting spirit doesn't show. Hiding her glory's fight makes her look sullen, makes her silent. She knows it arouses her mother's suspicion. But looking happy, or trying to be happy, that would make her suspicious as well.

Her glory tells her not to worry but she can't help it. The week is going too fast. The work hours fly by, the nights disappear. Friday and the weekend loom before her and she knows she's not ready for either of them. She's trying. She's working. She's fighting. There's just not enough time.

Since her mother spoke to her the younger sister has been watching. She watches like her mother does but she sees more. She hears more. They share a bathroom. The sister listens while her older sister takes a shower, flushes the toilet. She's hearing more than the sound of water and she knows what's going on. She realises now what her mother suspected. Why her mother is so insistent when it comes to her sister's food. She understands what is happening but she's not sure what to do.

The younger sister walks up to her.

I know what you've been doing.

She is surprised. She sometimes forgets her sister.

What?
In the bathroom. I know what you're doing.

She doesn't know what to say.

And I know you snuck out of the house. Ages ago. When you first met Daniel.
So?
I lied for you then.
So?

The younger sister doesn't know what to say. She was expecting her sister to crumple. To confess. To ask for her silence. She doesn't know what to do. She wants her to stop. She knows it's bad. She wants to be made a part of

88

it. To share it with her so she doesn't have to tell her mother. But her sister offers nothing and she doesn't know what to do. She is quiet so long the older sister walks away.

She doesn't spend much time thinking about what her sister has said. It doesn't matter. Not when the week is slipping away and she's still as fat as she was when it started. She thinks about jogging to work but she'd be too sweaty when she arrived. So she starts to run home instead of catching the bus. She walks the last few blocks so she doesn't look puffed when she gets home. She knows it must look strange. A girl in a checkout uniform running down the street. At least the uniform has stretched now. It's looser around her hips and stomach and moves independently of her as she runs. But it still must look strange. She doesn't care. The week is slipping away.

She is ashamed of her behaviour with her older sister. She goes over the conversation in her mind and realises she approached it all wrong. Sees how she could have done it better, how she had an opportunity and how she messed it up. Her sister makes a point to avoid her now, more than she did before. It upsets her. She tells herself it doesn't but it does. She tells herself over and over she doesn't care. But she does. She knows her sister will despise her but she does care. She can't fight it. So she tells her mother about the bathroom noises.

It's Thursday. She is filled with a feeling of dread. She can't back out and she can't get thin in one day. Her glory is fighting for her but she knows she's lost. This time she's lost. Mandy has a different lunch hour and she is relieved she doesn't have to have a conversation with her. Her glory tells her to hope. To hope that maybe when she wakes up on Friday morning she will be thin. If she's careful not to let any food into her stomach. If she exercises really hard. Maybe her glory will be right.

The mother waits for her daughter to come home from work. She has come home early so she can catch her daughter the moment she walks into the house. By the time her younger daughter told her this morning the elder was already on her way to work. She thought about going to get her from work. She thought about calling her husband, consulting with him. But she hasn't done anything. She has spent her day sitting and worrying. Spent her day planning. And now, she hopes, she has worked out what to do.

As soon as she walks in the door she sees her mother. Like she's ready to pounce. She is taken by surprise and without really knowing why, turns to run out the door. Her mother catches her by the arm and leads her to the car. They don't speak as they both try to control their anger and their fear. She wants to speak. She wants to stop what's going on. She wants to say you can't do this to me. Her glory is telling her, she can't do this to you. She remains silent. There doesn't seem to be any room for conversation in the car.

She wants to speak. She can see how frightened her daughter is. She wants to reassure her. Tell her everything is going to be all right and this is for her own good. But she's afraid she'll say the wrong thing, knowing there is no right thing to say. When they get to the hospital she looks at her daughter's face. She can see the fear and the rage in her eyes. She wants to say one thing. One thing that will help make it better.

It's for your own good.

It's the best she can do.

The hospital feels familiar as she walks down the corridor. Her glory is crying, you don't belong here, and she knows it's right. Even though it's familiar, she belongs at the supermarket now. The hospital should be behind her. They receive her with very few questions and admit her quickly. They tell her it's for observation. She tells them she can only stay the night. She has work tomorrow. They smile at her and say, *we'll see.*

She tries to convince them it's all a mistake. She tries to talk to them with reason so they'll let her go. So she can keep her glory.

I'm not sick.

The nurse just smiles at her.

My mother worries too much. She over reacts.

The nurse smiles again and tells her that the doctor will be in to see her soon.

She gets worried waiting in the hospital for the doctor. They want to take her glory away. She'll lose her job because they'll keep her here as long as they can. She'll lose her glory because the doctors, her mother, will take it away. Her mother comes into the room and announces that she is leaving. She waits for her to say something, but she has nothing to say. Her mother tries to kiss her. She turns her face away.

I'm doing this for you. One day you'll thank me.

And then she is gone.

As the mother walks away from her daughter and out of the hospital she wonders if she's done the right thing. If her daughter will ever forgive her for interfering in her life. She thinks about all the things she could have said and wonders why it is only clichés that come out of her mouth when she is faced with her daughter. She wonders if these were the things her mother said to her and if she'll ever think of something original to say. Something that would make things better rather than worse.

They keep her in the hospital until Saturday. Her mother rings the supermarket on Friday morning to say she won't be in. She hasn't told her mother about the party on Saturday night. She can't go anyway, they were going to make the plan at work. She wouldn't know where to go and she doesn't have Mandy's phone number. They wouldn't let her go anyway. Not after the hospital. She is disappointed but also relieved. Now she'll have more time to get thin. If Mandy asks her again.

In the hospital they weigh her, they measure her, they pinch her flesh. They tell her she is underweight but it's not dangerous. Yet. They ask about her diet and she explains the list. They nod their heads sympathetically. She lies about exercising, she lies about lunch. She stands ashamed as they look over her body. She wants to say it's not finished yet. We're still working. But she can't. She knows it would be the wrong thing to say. All she can do is wait, hold on to her glory as best she can and hope it will be over soon.

Dinner on Saturday night is tense. Every time she looks at her mother she sees the party she could be at. She sees the fun she could have been having and she sees that her glory could be growing. Instead she is forced to sit at this table. No one speaking. Her mother and sister watching her plate. Watching the fork move to her mouth. She has to eat it. There's no way out. She hopes it will make a point so she eats everything on her plate. She says no to more but she eats everything on her plate. Her mother doesn't care about her point. She has a point of her own. She has to leave the bathroom door open. Until her weight becomes normal. She says her weight is normal, they let her out of the hospital didn't they? But her mother just repeats herself. She has to leave the bathroom door open.

The sister is frightened. Her sister must know it was her. Must blame her. She sits at the dinner table scared to make a sound. Scared to attract attention to herself. She thinks if she starts to speak, her sister will attack her. Will turn the rage she has in her eyes, now focused on her mother, to her. She wouldn't know what to do if her sister yelled at her. She would deserve it. She shouldn't have told. She didn't know what else to do. She didn't think her mother would take her back to the hospital. She thought they would just talk to her. But now, looking at her family around the dinner table, she realises no one knows what to say.

On Monday she goes to work. Her mother doesn't

want her to but she doesn't have a choice. The hospital let her go. Her mother can't hold her back now. The hospital said she was all right and she can't miss another day of work. They could fire her. She can't miss seeing Mandy either. She might forget her and not bother inviting her to another party. Her glory is stronger now. It has been to the hospital and come back intact. Her glory tells her to go to work. Tells her that Mandy will ask her to another party. Her glory tells her nothing can stop them now and she is starting to believe it.

At lunch Mandy tells her about the party. It's hard for her to picture. She's only been to a few high school parties. Mandy says it would have been more fun if she was there and that her friends were disappointed. They wanted to meet her. She says she was disappointed too but she was sick and there was no way her mother would have let her go. Mandy nods like she understands and says parents suck. Mandy says as soon as she can afford it she's getting her own place and she remembers her fantasy house. Mandy says there's another party this weekend and she should come. She looks surprised. Mandy laughs. There's always another party and she is relieved. Her mother didn't spoil everything. It's going to be all right.

When she tells her parents about her weekend plans

she notices her sister staring at her. She has noticed since the hospital her sister is always staring at her. She ignores it. She tells her parents she's going to stay at her friend's house. They are surprised. She hasn't told them about Mandy. Her mother wants to refuse. They'll let her shut the bathroom door. She won't eat properly there. Her father intervenes.

For one night. Let her close the bathroom door for one night.

And so she is going.

What can a mother do. She feels like some old Italian grandmother. A Jewish mother stereotype. Eat, eat she says every time she sees her daughter. But the daughter doesn't respond, doesn't even look at her, she just goes to her room. At dinner she watches as her daughter eats half of what is on her plate and returns to her room. She watches her put her knife and fork down and she says is that all you're eating, before her daughter can walk away. What about a little more potato? Every time she hears herself saying these things she wants to stop. Take the words back. At the hospital they told her not to pressure her this way but she can't help it. She doesn't know what else to do. She can't do nothing. She has to say something. So she says eat, eat.

The supermarket is the busiest she's ever seen it. It's a week and a half before Christmas now and every day is spent at the checkout, hour after hour of scanning and packing and taking money and giving change. The week goes so quickly that before she realises what's happening she is planning what to wear and walking over to Mandy's house.

She's never been to a party like it. Everyone is smoking and drinking. She looks around at the crowd and knows she's the youngest person there. Of course she had nothing to wear to a party like this. She borrowed clothes from Mandy and now, looking around at the other girls, she's glad she did.

Mandy introduces her to her friends. She tries to remember all their names but it's like Mandy knows everyone and she finds it hard to keep up. Some of them look at her like she's just a kid and go back to their conversation. Others stop and say something. She likes the people who talk to her. They begin to make her feel like she belongs.

They stand in the lounge room and she watches the people around her. The music is loud and throbbing. People lean against the walls talking and nodding at each other. People pile onto the couches falling onto each other and laughing. Two girls dance in the middle of the room like they are the only ones there. Mandy says something to her, she doesn't really hear what, but she nods her head and Mandy leaves. And then she is standing alone at a party, surrounded by people she doesn't know.

She doesn't notice Steve as he moves to stand beside her. She's watching the two girls dancing.

World of their own.

She turns to look at him. She remembers him as one of the people Mandy introduced her to when they arrived. Steve. She's pleased she remembers his name.

What?
WORLD OF THEIR OWN.

He points to the two girls. She smiles.

So you work with Mandy?

She nods.

He nods.

They watch the girls for a while.

I'm going outside for some fresh air. You want to come?

She understands what he says more from his actions than from being able to hear his words but she smiles and nods again. He takes her hand and leads her through the house and out into the backyard.

She's thinking about his hand, holding her hand.

She finds it strange. A stranger holding her hand. And she likes it. It makes her feel safer than standing alone in the lounge room. Suddenly she's outside, surrounded by cool air, quiet. He looks at her and smiles.

Better?
Yeah.

He doesn't let her hand go now that they are outside. She doesn't take hers away from his either. She looks around for Mandy but can't see her. He notices.

She's down the back with Pete.

Mandy never mentioned Pete. She wants to ask, who's Pete, but she stays silent and wonders what she should do.

Don't worry.

She wonders why Steve is still hanging around. She can't be any fun. She hasn't even said anything.

I'll look after you.

Her glory tells her he likes her but she finds it hard to believe. He has to be at least eighteen. Why would he want to talk to her?

The mother finds it hard to sleep that Saturday night. She's waiting for a phone call. Waiting to hear her daughter walk through the door. Knowing she won't hear either. She looks at her sleeping husband. She can't understand how this doesn't bother him. But they have discussed it.

She's only fifteen.
We have to trust her. Even if we're wrong. We have to try.
They aren't just staying at Mandy's. They're going somewhere.
Probably.
What if she gets into trouble?
What if she doesn't?
She's not well.
It's too late now. She's gone. We just have to trust her.
I can't.
I know.

She wants to wake him. Have the discussion again. It won't make her feel any better but maybe it will make him feel worse. Maybe it will stop him sleeping. She can't do it. It would just cause a fight. She settles back into the bed and prepares for a long night.

He pulls out a hand rolled cigarette and lights it. He offers it to her.

I don't smoke.
It's not tobacco.
Oh.

She feels stupid. She doesn't know what to do so she takes what he is offering and puts it to her lips. She doesn't cough. It makes her feel cool. Maybe he'll think she's done it before. He takes it from her and smokes it for a while before handing it back. She coughs this time. She looks at Steve. He hasn't seemed to notice. He's reaching for the joint again with a vague look in his eyes.

She doesn't really feel the effects of the joint. She feels the smoke in her lungs. It makes her chest tight. She doesn't feel more relaxed. She feels tired and tense. She hopes Mandy will appear soon and rescue her. Maybe they can go back to her place and talk about the night. Giggle and behave like friends. Mandy could tell her about Pete and ask her about Steve. She wouldn't know what to say about Steve. She could only say he held her hand and shared his joint with her. She feels like that's enough for one night but Mandy is nowhere to be seen and she's still with Steve.

Let's go.

She's surprised to hear his voice.

Where?
Somewhere quieter, darker.

She doesn't know what to do so she agrees and he

leads her deeper into the backyard. The grass is long and patchy. He lies back into it.

You just going to stand there?

She sits down next to him.

The stars look great tonight.

She looks up at the sky. They don't look that special to her.

Yeah.

She wants to say something, start a conversation but she doesn't know what Steve would want to talk about. What they could have in common. She is about to ask him what he does when suddenly he is kissing her and pushing her back into the grass. It's not like when Daniel used to kiss her. This is different. More. She doesn't know what. Just more.

His hands are all over her body. Feeling her fat. She stops thinking about trying to kiss him back and starts worrying about her body. He notices the tension in her body.

I'm going too fast for you.

But she says no, even though she wants him to stop. She doesn't want him to leave her alone at the party. He stops anyway. He lies next to her, propped up on one elbow and he looks at her. It makes her nervous but he smiles. He tells her she's pretty. Then he jumps to his feet. He grabs her hand and pulls her up next to him. He kisses her. Lightly this time and her glory responds. He thinks she's pretty. He takes her hand.

Let's go find Mandy and Pete.

Mandy smiles when she sees Steve holding her hand.

We're going to crash at Pete's.

It takes her a while to realise that she means her too. They're all going to crash at Pete's. She doesn't even know Pete. Steve smiles.

That's great. I'm crashing there too.

And she smiles at him but inside she's scared. She looks at Pete. He looks like he doesn't care who crashes. They all crowd into Pete's car. There are six of them. They tell her she's the smallest so she has to sit on Steve's lap. She wonders if they're making fun of her.

Pete's place is dark and damp. There are people there when they arrive. They're sitting on the couch looking half asleep. They barely notice the six of them walk in. The other two guys who were in the car sit on the couch with the others and watch the

TV. Mandy smiles at her and leaves with Pete. They walk into one of the rooms and close the door. She wonders if she should sit down and watch the TV. Steve takes her hand.

Come on.

Where?

We'll crash in Mark's room.

Won't he mind?

Naah, he's at his girlfriend's.

She's made a decision. Christmas dinner. The whole family, no friends, just the four of them. They'll spend the day together. They'll open presents and eat good food. They'll have fun and talk about good times. Maybe get out the photo album. She won't mind if the elder daughter doesn't eat but of course she will because the food will be special. Maybe the girls could have a glass of wine. They won't talk about hospital bills. They won't talk about eating and ideal weights. They'll just have fun. The four of them.

She day dreams about Steve kissing her. His lips are soft and when they touch her lips, her stomach muscles tighten. She day dreams about him kissing her and it's beautiful. Perfect. In her mind, as she watches him kiss her, his hair is thicker and face finer and she is thinner with her hair falling all the way down her back.

She likes the day dream. Better than the night she crashed at Pete's. She feels awful about that night. Mandy told her that Steve really likes her but she doesn't believe her. Not after that night. She thinks she did it all wrong. But then he's waiting for her after work. She's embarrassed that he sees her in her uniform but he doesn't seem to care. He kisses her and touches her as if he really likes her and it makes her feel good. It makes her feel wanted. They go back to Pete's and lie around his place. He says he's crashing there for a while. Until he finds his own place. He touches her and kisses her again. He tells her all about himself. The good and the bad and she starts to think she's falling in love.

When she gets home so late she has to lie. She says she was looking for Christmas presents. Her mother looks surprised but accepts her answer. She goes to her room, stares at the ceiling. She thinks about Steve and her glory and she begins to form a plan.

She announces her plan at breakfast. Money is tight, always tight since the hospital but she doesn't care. It's Christmas and they're going to have a good one. She's not asking her family, she's telling them. Because it's her family and she wants it to be good. Good for all of them. She tells them at breakfast and they all nod their heads but they don't look happy. She wants to slap them. Slap them all. She wants to say, can't you see I'm trying? Don't you see how much I do, how much I worry?

Well you could try and look a little happy.

And the three of them look at her, different kinds of smiles on all their faces, but smiles all the same and she begins to feel a little better.

She doesn't mind sitting through Christmas dinner. She knows it's the last one. By new year, she'll be gone.

Three

I'm standing on the edge of a cliff.

Below me I can see the ocean. Behind me are my parents and sister sitting on a picnic blanket. They're eating the lunch my mother has prepared. But not me.

I am standing. Standing on the edge of a cliff staring down at the water below.

There's a coolness in my hand. I look to see what it is. I'm holding a gun. I turn it over and examine it from all sides. I point it at my body and play with the trigger. Blood begins to run down my legs, on to the ground, over the cliff edge. I look to see where it's coming from but I can't tell. I wonder how the gun came to be in my hands.

I turn to look at my family. They're still eating. They can't see the blood.

I think about calling to them. I think about drawing their attention to the gun, to the blood.

But instead I stand. On the edge of a cliff, gun in hand. I watch my blood drip into the ocean.

The fat girl is moving through her life. Striding through its years. Inhaling the days, exhaling the nights. The fat girl is moving through her life. The fat girl is taking it in hand, putting it in her mouth. The fat girl knows where it's at, seen where it's been. The fat girl is moving through her life. The fat girl is changing her world, upping the stakes, measuring the boundaries and drawing lines. She is reaching out and drawing in, taking in, putting out. The fat girl is moving through her life.

She didn't take much when she left her family home. A few clothes. Her uniform of course. As she looked around her room deciding what to take, most of it looked like junk. Anything to do with school was now useless. Anything that carried memories, she didn't want. She couldn't imagine walking into Pete's with her old doll. She took her small pink rabbit, hidden deep in her bag.

Pete's place is a mess. Always. It has four bedrooms, one bathroom, a kitchen, lounge room and not much of a backyard. Pete's room is the biggest. That's why they call it Pete's place. They crash in Mark's room. He's practically living with his girlfriend, just hasn't moved his stuff yet. The other two guys, Luke and Dave, are stoned most of the time and either hang out in their rooms or watch TV.

When she first started crashing there she used to try

and clean it up. When she got home from work she'd collect the rubbish, do the dishes, empty the ashtrays and sweep a bit. By the time she went to bed it would be getting messy again and by the time she got home from work the next day it would be the same as the day before. Now she doesn't bother. Sometimes she picks up the rubbish or throws out the rotting food. It doesn't really matter anymore, she and Steve are talking about getting a place of their own.

She thought Christmas went quite well. They did everything like she planned and the food turned out fine. She asked him, do you think it went all right? Do you think the girls liked it? And he smiled at her and said yes because he knew it was the right thing to say. She asked her daughters, did you have a good day? One said yes straight away but the other needed prompting.

Well did you?

And she said yes thank you, and the mother felt relief. The voice was a little cold and not really there but she saw it as a sign that she was trying. Yes, she thought, Christmas went well and she started to feel courageous. She believed after Christmas, things were going to get better.

She imagined she would go into her parents' room before she left, stand at the doorway and say, I'm leaving, I can't stand it here any more. But when it came to the moment she lacked the courage. She didn't even leave a note. She just left. Walked out of the house. When she got halfway down the block she turned back to look at it. She almost expected to see her sister, standing at her bedroom window, watching her go. But the house was dark and she walked away thinking she would never go back.

They didn't think anything of it when she wasn't there at the table in the morning. She rarely was. After the father left for work and the sister is almost ready to go to her friends, the mother begins to get worried. She wants to say, go and see if your sister is all right, but she holds the words back and goes herself. When she gets to her daughter's bedroom door she is nervous, preparing herself for some sort of argument, although about what she has no idea. And then there is nothing. No daughter, no argument. She tries to tell herself that it's okay, she's somewhere else in the house but at that moment she knows, she's gone. And worse, she doesn't understand why.

She likes crashing at Pete's with Steve. There's never any food in the place. No one asks her if she ate lunch, no one even thinks there's anything strange if she doesn't eat dinner. It's just more for them and she likes it that way. She likes being with Steve too. He makes her feel special. They don't do much. They talk about it. They talk about going to see a movie or something but they're saving their money for a place of their own. Sometimes they get videos and if the other guys aren't there they take the TV and video into their room, Mark's room, and watch them in bed.

She doesn't think much of sex but she's proud she's having it. At first she clung to the pain. She remembered her days in the hospital when her pain was her glory. But it doesn't hurt anymore and she doesn't miss it. She gets her glory from other sources now. She tries to do things in bed to please Steve. Sometimes she worries she's not good enough and he might look for another girl, someone more experienced. But Steve always kisses her after sex and tells her she's beautiful. And he always comes back for more.

She didn't know what to do. She walked back to her youngest and said, your sister isn't there. Her daughter is surprised. No one expected she would leave.

Do you know where she might be?

She shakes her head.

Think.

The mother wanted to yell but controlled her voice.

Think where she might have gone.
What about Mandy's?

The girl from work. But they didn't know where she lived.
Didn't even have a phone number.

The new year is over and they haven't said anything at work. She starts to feel safe in her job but doesn't have the courage to ask. Mandy says she doesn't care if they fire her. She'd just get a job somewhere else. She wants a better job anyway. In a CD shop or video store or something. But she doesn't want another job. She's just starting to feel comfortable in this one. It's different for Mandy. Mandy can fit in anywhere.

She called work and said she wasn't coming in. She
called her husband.

She's gone.
What?
Last night I think. She left.
Where?
I don't know.
Jesus.

She waited on the phone, hoping he would have an
answer but he didn't know what to say. At least when she
was sick, in the hospital, they knew where she was.

I don't want to call the police.

She had pictured her daughter, kicking and screaming, being dragged back into the house.

Are you all right?

She was surprised he thought to ask.

I don't know.

And she didn't.

I'll try and be home early.

She spent the day wandering around the house. She watched TV, just staring at the screen trying not to imagine the worst. She knew she should go to the supermarket but she couldn't bring herself to do it. She sent her youngest instead. She didn't know what else to do.

She continues to day dream about Steve at work. Sometimes she imagines they are married. She sees Steve getting a good job and them living together in a nice place. Maybe building her dream house. Sometimes she imagines they're making up after a big fight and he is begging her not to leave him. Telling her he can't live without her. They haven't had a fight yet. They don't have anything to fight about.

She begins to tell him things. At night, when they are lying in bed and not yet asleep, she tells him things she didn't think she would. She tells him about the hospital, about school. She tells him about being adopted and her list of food. He just listens, never asks her questions. Sometimes she thinks he isn't listening at all, his mind is somewhere else, thinking about work or if there's anything left to eat. She doesn't let it stop her. It makes her tell him more. And if she asks if she's boring him he tells her no and she can hear the smile in his voice. She stops talking then anyway. Sometimes he smokes a joint while she is talking. She doesn't share it with him now. It makes her hungry.

She waits for her sister outside the supermarket. Her sister doesn't seem surprised to see her. She doesn't ask her what she is doing there or anything. She says hi, like she expects her to be there. She doesn't know what to say but her sister does.

Tell them I'm okay but I'm not going home.

She still doesn't know what to say. She wants to know where she's living and who she's living with. She wants to know why she left.

Will you call them? So they can hear for themselves you're all right?

Yeah, okay. When I'm ready. I've got to go now. I'm meeting someone.

She wants to say who? Who are you meeting? But instead she says goodbye and watches her sister walk away.

Mandy and Pete are having a fight. They're in Pete's room and the door is shut but everyone in the house can hear it. She's embarrassed for Mandy. Pete's been unfaithful. She knew about it but Steve made her promise not to tell so what could she do. She wants to leave the house so she doesn't have to hear but Steve is watching something on TV and doesn't want to go anywhere. She can tell he's enjoying the argument. She goes out anyway. On her own. Just for a walk. She walks for as long as she can and when she comes back the house is quiet. Pete is watching TV with the other guys and Mandy has gone.

She said to tell you she's fine and she'll call soon.

Where is she staying?

I don't know.

Why did she leave?

She didn't say anything else.

And what else is there to say. Her mother tells herself at least she's all right but that doesn't make her feel any better. It makes her feel worse. Here they are all worried

and anxious and she's off doing what ever she wants.
They're still paying the hospital bills and they don't even
have a daughter to show for it. She looks at her younger
child, sitting quietly, watching her.

Well I guess that's that.

She says this because she can't think of anything else to
say.

Mandy never spoke to her again. Not after her fight
with Pete. It made work uncomfortable and she
started to avoid the lunch room. It turned out only
to be for a few days but they felt like very long days.
Mandy left the supermarket soon after she had the
fight with Pete. She heard some of the other women
talking about how she had got a job in a music
store, like she always wanted. She was pleased
Mandy got what she wanted. And she was relieved
she could now go into the lunch room without the
fear of an icy stare from her.

Mandy fighting with Pete and leaving also means
she's lost another friend. It makes her think about
Samantha and Cherie. She started to avoid Samantha when she was seeing Daniel because she knew
Samantha didn't approve. They were friends before
the hospital and it's hard for her to remember why.
Cherie gave her scotch on the roof and helped her
get a job at the supermarket but she hasn't spoken

to her since. She wonders if she should call her. She would probably be impressed that she was living out of home with her boyfriend. But she doesn't call her. Instead she goes back to Pete's place, the only girl there now. She sits with the guys, watching them eat and swap jokes and she begins to miss Mandy.

It's quiet at home without her. They sit silently around the table eating. When the silence gets too much they force themselves to have a conversation. They try to avoid talking about the empty chair. Sometimes they do talk about it though. Sometimes they can't stop themselves. Those times are a great relief for the sister. She thinks maybe it's painful for her mother and the mother just feels like she failed and the father doesn't know what to think. He isn't happy that they haven't tried to do anything. That they haven't called the police. That they haven't caught her outside the supermarket and forced her to come home. His wife says she has to want to come home. Otherwise she'll just leave again, and he can see the sense in her words. But he finds it frustrating. Just sitting there, not knowing what to do.

She doesn't tell Steve about missing Mandy. Instead she questions him about himself. He's all she has now. When they first met he started to tell her about himself but then he just stopped. She thought he didn't want to talk about himself any more and so she didn't ask him any questions. But now, when she does question him, she realises he has nothing much to say. His parents are divorced and he doesn't see his dad much. His mum is cool about him living out of home. He doesn't have any brothers or sisters. He says one day he'll take her around to meet his mum and she can't imagine what that would be like.

Steve works in the mail room of a law firm in the city. He goes to work in a tie. When she first started living with him she was impressed by that. She liked to watch him tie his tie in the morning. He used to talk about the job, about the potential for him there. He doesn't talk about it much any more. She doesn't ask him why. She just assumes it's like her job. There's not much to say.

School has started again but after school she goes to the supermarket and waits outside for her sister. She's nervous and her words rush out as soon as she sees her.

When are you coming home?

Her sister doesn't say anything.

Mum really worries about you.
I can't go back there. Not to live.
Why don't you just try? Just give it another go?
You don't understand.

She's right. She doesn't understand. But she wants to.

121

I have to go.

Why don't you come home, just for dinner or something?
Just so they can see you're all right.

Maybe.

When?
I don't know.

Thursday?
Okay.

And then she leaves and the sister can't believe she won.

Mark has finally moved out of the house and into
his girlfriend's place and they officially get the room.
He leaves his bed and clothes rack for them to use.
They don't talk about getting their own place any
more. Steve starts to spend his money more freely
and she begins to think she should be doing the
same. But Steve spends his money on dope and
alcohol and she's not that interested in either of
those. She does drink. She gets drunk. But she
doesn't care about it. She doesn't look forward to it.
It makes her feel too sick in the morning. She continues to do it though because it helps her to enjoy
herself. To get over the shyness she often feels. She'd
like to spend her money on clothes. But she doesn't
have a girlfriend to go with. She's never been shopping alone. She's not sure she'd like it.

When she gets home her mother is there. She doesn't know how to tell her the news. Her mother can see it on her face.

What?
I went to the supermarket.
Oh.
I asked her to come over for dinner and she said yes.

She sees the surprise in her mother's eyes and the smile on her mother's face.

Thursday.

She watches as her mother walks to the cupboard to see what food they have. She knows she's already planning the meal. She hopes she's done the right thing.

She tells Steve about Thursday night as soon as he gets home.

You want me to go with you?

But she shakes her head. She can't think of anything worse.

She tells him as soon as he gets home.

She's coming over for dinner. On Thursday.
Great. That's great.
I don't know what to do.

You don't have to do anything.

She doesn't know what he means. She's thinking of course I have to do something. She's my daughter. I have to hug her, hold her, make sure she's all right. I have to convince her to stay.

She walks slowly to her parents' house. She thinks about what to say to them. She thinks about what they are going to say to her. She wonders why she's going back at all and she doesn't really have an answer. Because her sister asked her. The house looks strange and familiar at the same time. She can't imagine living there again. Waking up in her old bed and sitting down to breakfast. Her mother, looking at her list, looking at her plate, looking at her body. She thinks about running, turning around and running away from the house. But she can't. She's too close now. She forces herself to walk to the front door.

On the way to the house she wondered if she should knock or use her key. She thought she should knock. It would be strange but it would make it clear she didn't want to live there any more. When she finally makes it to the front door there is no decision to make. The door is open. Her sister is waiting for her. She leads her into the house, into the kitchen, she smiles the whole time. Her mother stands nervously

124

by the stove. She smiles too but her smile is a little forced. No one knows what to say.

At dinner she makes her announcement.

I'm living with my boyfriend now. And some of his friends.

It sounded better in her head than it does when she speaks it. There is silence after this statement. Her father clears his throat.

Really?

She can tell he's trying to sound casual.

And what does he do?
He works in the city. At a law firm. In the mail room.

She thought about lying but decided against it. There was nothing wrong with working in a mail room.

And what about you? You still at the supermarket?

They know she still works there. That's how her sister keeps finding her. She doesn't point this out. She recognises the effort her father is making.

Yeah.
How's it going?
Fine.

She hasn't said anything all night. She's trying to smile. She's trying to think of something to say. She thought it would be wonderful to see her family, all of her family, around the table again. But it just makes her angry. She's afraid if she opens her mouth the anger will come out and she won't be able to stop it. So she leaves it inside of her. Going around and around until she is screaming on the inside. Screaming, what right do you have to put us through this? She wants to remind her about the hospital bills, remind her of what they went through. She wants her to know that being adopted doesn't give you the right to leave your family any time you choose.

She doesn't know why she came. She wonders how long she has to sit at the table. Sit while her mother stays silent, her father makes casual conversation and her sister smiles like everything is perfect. Pete's place is looking like paradise now. She doesn't care about the mess, about the guys just lying around never interested in doing much except getting drunk, getting stoned and watching TV. She wants to go back there. They don't question her life there. They don't look at her expectantly, waiting for her to say something to make everything all right.

I'm sorry. I'm very tired.

Everyone is surprised that the mother has spoken at all.

I guess this was the wrong night to have you here.

No one knows what to say. The mother knows she has said the wrong thing and tries to make it better.

You're welcome to stay the night if you want.

She has to leave. Now. She stands.

Thank you. And thank you for dinner. I have to go now.

She walks as fast as she can to the front door. Her sister and father follow. Her mother remains sitting at the table, wondering if she should start clearing up.

When they reach the door her sister asks her to consider staying. Just for tonight. She shakes her head. She can't. Her father asks for a phone number and she writes it down on a piece of paper for him. She's not really sure why her sister looks so upset but it makes her nervous and she walks away as fast as she can.

She is relieved when she gets to Pete's place, her place, that the guys are drinking. She helps herself to a large glass of cask wine. Steve asks her how dinner went. She says fine because she doesn't want to talk about it in front of everyone else and she hopes Steve will remember to ask her about it when they go to bed.

They go to bed silently. She doesn't know what to say, what he's thinking. She knows she ruined the dinner. She knows tonight is her fault. Maybe they had a chance to get her back tonight. Maybe she ruined their chance. Maybe it was their last one. She hates to think of her living with a man. It's not legal. She knows it's not legal. They could force her back. She's not even sixteen. But when she pictures the fight they would have to get her back into the house and to keep her in the house she knows it would only make things worse.

She wakes up in the morning with a headache and a sick feeling in her stomach and the knowledge that something has changed. She goes to work complaining and comes home hoping the guys are drinking. Hoping there will be a party, even a small party, so she can stop thinking about the dinner. About her mother's silence and her sister's tears. The guys don't disappoint her. She even has a slice of pizza. She can't remember the last time she had pizza. It makes her feel free. And then fat.

Pete has a new girlfriend. Her name's Carol but everyone calls her Titch. Because of her last name, which is something long and European, that no one can pronounce. She's seen Titch around at parties but has never really spoken to her before. They meet in the kitchen one morning when she is on her way to work. Titch is a few years older than her and smoking a joint. It's her day off. You don't really get days off when you work in a supermarket. Just weekends. Titch works in a café so she doesn't always get weekends. They talk for a while. Titch offers her the joint and she takes it because she wants to be friends. She's missed having a friend. She gets to work late and stoned.

They sit around the table in silence. She's angry with her parents, both of them.

You made her go.

They've had this conversation before and her parents aren't interested in having it again.

She left because she wanted to leave.

But she knows that's not true. Her mother's silence and all of her father's questions forced her out of the house. She's worried her sister won't speak to her again. If she goes to the supermarket to see her she may be ignored because the dinner was so bad. She doesn't want to lose her sister. She doesn't like feeling like an only child. But now, because of her parents, she doesn't think her sister will ever return.

Titch is still there when she gets home from work. She gets changed quickly and joins her in the lounge room. Pete took the day off but is sleeping in his room. The other guys haven't come home yet. Titch talks about where she lives. She lives in a place where she doesn't have to pay rent. A squat. She says it's okay but there's some tension there at the moment with some of the people. That's why she's spent the day here. She doesn't feel like going back to that yet. She can understand how Titch feels. Except that she knows she will never go back.

They drink wine and smoke a joint while they sit in the lounge room waiting for Pete to wake up and Steve to get home. She tells Titch about being adopted and the hospital. Titch doesn't look at her like she feels sorry for her. She looks at her like these are things that everyone has to go through and she is relieved.

Steve is surprised to see her laughing and stoned on the couch with Titch. She doesn't care. She's enjoying herself. Drinking and smoking with Titch reminds her of being on the roof with Cherie. She realises how much she has missed having a friend since Mandy and Pete split up.

Titch wakes Pete up and the four of them go to the pub where they drink beer and play pool until closing time. She knows she will feel awful in the morning but she doesn't care. She's alone now. The baby in the basket on the doorstep all over again. Only now it's real. And now she can look after herself. Choose her own life, her own fun. They buy more beer and take it home with them. She can't drink anymore but she stays up with them. Talking and joking until it's so late she wonders if there's any point in sleeping before work.

It's surprising how quickly the house returns to calm when she is gone and when the younger daughter stops talking about the dinner. They stop speaking about her. They have a routine, they all know the boundaries. No one disturbs any of the lines. No one wants to anymore. Sometimes the younger daughter wants to shout her name, wants to question them, push them against the wall and say why don't you do something? But she remains silent, like them. She doesn't really want to disturb the silence, she almost likes the calm even though she finds it frustrating sometimes. They have found a way of existing without her sister in that calm, frustrating, silence.

She has forgotten about her glory. When it appears, it reminds her of its presence, she realises it's always there. It just hasn't been her focus. But now it's taking charge. Threatening to leave. Her glory tells her she's going to make herself sick. Her body can't take all the beer. They're going to put her in hospital. And then they'll take her glory away again and she'll have to fight all over to get it back. She doesn't want to stop drinking. She doesn't want to look after her body, to have to think all the time about her list and what's good for her. And even though she hasn't been thinking about her glory much lately, she knows she doesn't want it to go.

When she gets home Steve is still in bed. He hasn't gone to work. She climbs in next to him wishing she could have been there all day too. He puts his arms around her. She likes it when he holds her. Sometimes he doesn't act like he cares about her. Sometimes she wonders if he thinks about her at all. But when he holds her she can let herself think that maybe he really does care about her. Maybe he loves her.

Steve earns more money than her. He can afford to take a day off. She always has to work, just to cover the rent and other living expenses. She can't imagine taking a day off. Her money is part of her glory. Even though the job is boring, the uniform is awful and the pay is low. It gives her money. It makes her independent. She doesn't know what she'd do without it.

Her sister is waiting for her when she finishes work. It's a Friday and she is anxious to get home. There's a party tonight and she wants to get ready for it. But her sister is there and she can't ignore her.

Why did you leave?

She asks the question in an angry voice. It surprises both of them.

I couldn't stay there.
You didn't even try.
I hate it there.
They're not coming after you. If that's what you want.

It never really occurred to her that they would force her back into the house.

I have to go.

Can I come with you? See where you live?

She's not ready for the question.

Maybe another time. Okay?

She walks away without waiting for an answer. She can't imagine her sister in the house. She can't imagine introducing her to Steve or any of the other guys. She doesn't fit into that picture. She belongs at home, with her parents. She doesn't want to mix the two up. It's too confusing.

Before they leave for the party she confesses to Titch that she doesn't want to drink tonight. She thinks it will make her boring if she doesn't drink and she's nervous when she tells her. Maybe she won't be any fun. Maybe Titch won't like her if she can't drink with her. Her glory makes her say it. She'd rather lose Titch than her glory. But when she tells her Titch smiles. She tells her not to worry. They have something else in mind.

Titch doesn't tell her what's been arranged. She thinks about asking as they make their way to the party but decides to trust her. She looks at Steve to see if he knows what's going to happen. He smiles at her which makes her think he does. She chooses to trust him too. She's been to parties at this house before. It makes her feel a little safer even though she keeps telling herself she has nothing to worry about.

Before they walk into the party Titch hands out what they are taking. She gives two to Steve and before he gives one to her he asks her if she's sure. She nods her head and together they swallow the pills. She feels no different and wonders how long it will take before something happens.

Later they tell her it's acid. It makes no difference to her, she doesn't know one drug from another. But after an hour or so she feels it. The drug takes hold of her from the inside and she doesn't know what's going on. She looks to the others to see if it's happening to them but they look just the same. Arguing and drinking, laughing at each other. She tries to control it but she feels so strange. And then she looks at Titch and Titch is laughing but she doesn't know why. She starts to laugh too. She can't help herself.

At home things are quiet. Life moves along at a moderate pace and they all get on with whatever they're doing. They don't talk about her sister. Well not to her anyway. She wonders if they talk about her at all. She hasn't told them she went to the supermarket. Or that she plans to go there again. Last time she thought she was doing the right thing, bringing her sister home, but they ruined it. She thought she could put the family together again. She thought she'd be the one to keep the family together. It never really occurred to her that her sister could be happy living away from home. But last time she saw her she did look happy. Thin, she looked thin, but not sick, not like she was in the hospital, and she looked happy.

She loses track of time. They're at the party for a while but then they want to go somewhere else. It's a group decision. They all feel the same. They need to go somewhere. They don't know where to go. They don't want to go back to the house. So they go to the park. The boys climb trees but she and Titch lie on their backs and look up at the sky. When she lies down she can feel the drug starting to move away. She starts to feel tired and sick. The drug comes back in waves but she knows it's leaving. She's happy to let it go. It's been fun but now she's getting tired. It's light by the time they leave the park and walk back to the house.

The next day is spent lying around the house. She hasn't been able to sleep yet. The others drink beer and smoke pot. She has some of the pot thinking it will help her sleep but it only makes her more alive. They get videos and continue to lie around the house. She thinks about the trip. She thinks she liked it. It didn't make her hungry like pot does. It took her to a different place. Made her a different person for a while. She still feels sick though. At least she is sick with other people feeling much the same. It's not like in the hospital where she was sick and alone. This is almost fun. Lying around, complaining together.

Sometimes she looks down at her wrist, admiring how the skin is tight across the bone. At work she watches her wrist working, pushing the groceries over the counter, taking money. She studies her arm as it moves towards her elbow, her admiration falls away as she sees her forearm begin to widen. She pulls at the extra flesh on her arms, checking if it's getting bigger or smaller, wondering if she'll ever be able to get rid of it. No matter how little she eats her body still widens out, gets bigger, when what she wants is for her whole body to be as tight as her wrists.

When she walks out of work her sister is there, waiting for her. Two or three times a week her sister is there. She wants to walk away, pretend she hasn't seen her or that she doesn't know her. But she's standing there waiting and there is no escape. She wants to tell her she's involved in her new life now and her family isn't part of that. But her sister is there, waiting for her, wanting to see where she lives and meet her boyfriend. She wonders if her parents are making her come but her sister says she doesn't even tell them. She doesn't know what to say to her, most of the time they just kind of stare at their feet, but her sister doesn't seem to care. She knows in a day or two when she's walking out of work, her sister will be there again. Waiting for her.

They start to try other drugs. Titch gets them. She thinks Titch has tried them all. Steve and Pete seem to know them pretty well too. She is willing to try whatever they offer. Sometimes the other guys in the house join in. Sometimes there are friends of friends there she doesn't know very well. There are always parties. Sometimes the parties are mid week and she has to turn up at work without sleep and feeling sick. On those days she tries to find her glory, she thinks her glory will be able to get her through the day. But her glory is harder and harder to find now and she just has to watch the hours tick by and try not to think of Steve, who's taken another day off and is probably asleep in their bed.

Acid has remained her favourite but she can't take it during the week. She knows the sickness on the following day would be too much for her to stand at the supermarket. She likes ecstasy too but it doesn't take her away like acid does. They had speed once but she didn't like that. It made her nervous and she didn't know what to do with her hands.

Her sister is following her.

I've been doing some reading.

It seems like her sister is always there now. Always waiting for her after work. She has no idea why.

Mum and Dad never really told me what was going on but I've been doing some reading and I think I understand now.

What are you talking about?

She can't be ignored. Her sister will follow her and follow her. She can't work out why she's so determined.

You can borrow the books if you want. They might help you.

I'm not sick any more.

But if you just read the books...

She stops walking.

I don't have time to read. I'm okay. Just go home.

Her sister stands there for a while. Shoulders dropping, face sad. Then she turns and walks away. She watches her leave. She refuses to feel guilty for upsetting her sister.

It happens on Saturday night. They go to a nightclub. She takes ecstasy because she doesn't like taking acid in nightclubs. They never used to go to nightclubs because she's underage but Titch organised a fake ID for her. She's only had to use it a few times. Titch has one too. She says no one's ever asked her for it but she carries it anyway. Just in case. The nightclub is crowded and the drug makes her feel serene and alive. She's dancing with Titch. She can't remember how long they've been dancing but she feels like she needs to rest. She walks away from the dance floor and remembers she hasn't seen Steve for a while. She begins to search for him.

She finds him in the alley next to the club with Pete. He's on the ground and looking pale. Pete tells her he's had too much speed. He asks her if she can look after him and she nods because she doesn't know what else to do and before she's aware of it Pete has gone. She sits with Steve. He tries to smile at her and she smiles back.

Do you want to go home?
Yes. But I can't move.

She rubs his back while he vomits and then she helps him to his feet. They walk slowly back to the house, stopping along the way for Steve to rest or vomit again. She feels like her drug left her body as soon as Pete left her alone with Steve but she knows it must still be there somewhere. She's grateful it's only ecstasy. If she were on acid she probably wouldn't be able to cope.

Luke and Dave are smoking pot and watching TV when they finally get home. They barely even look up as she walks Steve through the room. She tries to get him to shower but he won't so she puts him in bed with a bucket in case he vomits again and she wipes his body with a wet cloth. She stays awake all night, just watching him. In the early hours of the morning she hears Titch and Pete come in. She hears them giggling as they go into their room and shut the door.

She feels strange the next day when she speaks to Titch and Pete. They ask her how Steve is and she says he's fine. She even makes a joke. They laugh and tell her about their night. She feels strange because she never expected something like this to happen. And if it was going to happen she didn't realise it would be her responsibility. That they would just leave her to take care of Steve. She thinks they probably knew there was nothing really wrong with him. Nothing sleep wouldn't fix. But she didn't know. She was scared. And she was on her own.

The father feels a great sense of loss without the elder daughter in the house. When she was in hospital, well then it was difficult, but at least she was still there. There's a silence in the house he finds hard to get used to. He tries to believe his daughter was always going to leave, no matter what they did, she was always going to leave. But he can't help feeling they've failed her.

She forces herself to go to work every day. In her head while she's working she calculates what she's earning, hour by hour. Their life style is becoming expensive. It takes away everything they earn. Last week Steve couldn't come up with his share of the rent because he'd spent it on the weekend. She had to give him the last of her savings. Her money has always been security for her since she left her parents' house. If something went wrong between her and Steve then she'd have her savings. That would help her through. The way her glory does. She tries not to worry too much about spending her savings. She tries to put her trust in Steve and in their relationship. It's true she feels closer to Steve since the other night. Like they got through something together. But he could turn around and leave her alone, just like Titch and Pete did.

He goes to see her. Like his younger daughter he stands outside of the supermarket and waits for her to finish work. He can tell she's surprised, that she doesn't know what to do. He has already thought of this. He suggests they go to a small park nearby where they can sit and talk. She seems anxious, like she needs to be somewhere but she agrees and he is relieved. They sit on a bench and watch the traffic and the people. He tries to get a sense of how she is. She doesn't give much away. But it is a relief for him just to see her. She tells him she's happy where she's living. Happy with her life. He doesn't know what to say to that. He wants to feel happy for her but he only feels a sense of loss.

Work becomes something she has to live through to get to the night, or the night after that, whenever the next party is planned. A party can be just the four of them or six or eight. On the weekends they're bigger, at other people's houses or sometimes they throw a party in their house. They prefer to go to other people's houses though. The responsibility, the noise, the police arriving if it goes too late or stays too loud, all of that can ruin their night. They get too anxious.

They'd rather let someone else worry about it. They just want to have fun.

She watches Steve more closely now. Looks at how much he's taking and what he's taking. She never says anything. She knows Steve wouldn't like it. But she watches. So she knows. So if it happens again she'll feel more prepared. Sometimes he catches her looking and she has to look away quickly or pretend she's about to kiss him. She starts to feel like her sister. Always watching, always waiting. She pulls her attention back to herself. Back to what she's taking. She concentrates on having fun.

The mother knows they have both been to see her. She tries not to think it's a conspiracy but she can't help believing it is. She can't help believing that they both blame her. She knows she won't go and see her. She wouldn't know what to say. And she won't be forced to stand outside a supermarket to see her own daughter. So she gets on with her job, gets on with looking after the house and the people left in it and tries to believe she is getting on with her life.

Steve is waiting for her when she gets home.

Lost my job.

He doesn't say anything else and she doesn't know how to respond. She's not surprised. He's been taking

143

too many days off. She told him he was taking too many days off. She looks at him, trying to work out if he's upset. He shrugs at her.

It's no big deal. I'll just go on the dole.

She doesn't know how much money that is. She wonders if it is enough.

I don't care. There was nowhere to go in that job. I need a job that'll take me somewhere.

It makes her wonder where she's going.

Since the night Steve got sick she's drifted away from Titch and Pete. Or they've drifted away from her. She's not really sure how it happened. They spend a lot of time in Pete's room. Sometimes they go to different parties on the weekends. Sometimes they all still hang out together but not like they used to. She blames Steve for getting sick. For making them look uncool. She wants to ask Titch about it. To say, is it because of Steve? Or is it because of me? She's afraid of the answer so she doesn't ask. Maybe she doesn't need other friends. Maybe Steve is all she needs.

When it becomes obvious that Titch and Pete are doing something that purposely excludes them, she asks Steve about it. Steve tells her they've gotten into a different drug. Just now and then and he didn't think she'd be interested. He didn't think it would be good for her. She's surprised he is protective of her like this. He hasn't tried to protect her before. She is angry that he has spoken for her. She doesn't even know what the drug is. And she is relieved that Titch and Pete have been avoiding her because of something Steve said, not because of anything they've done.

It's like Titch and Pete have a secret and she's not allowed to know what it is. She hates it. She wants to be part of the secret. Part of the special group like they were when they took acid. She continues to question Steve about it. He shrugs her off like it's nothing special but she can't leave it alone. She doesn't want to be left out because of her body or because of her age. She wants to be part of them.

Steve tells her she wouldn't like it because it's like being stoned. Really stoned. But she doesn't care. Even he's tried it and admits he likes it. She tells him to stop protecting her. She tells him that's not what he's for. He's surprised. She can see it on his face. She's never spoken to him like that before. He relents and tells her he'll arrange to get some so she can try it, insisting all the time that she won't like it. She doesn't care. She doesn't care if she hates it. She just doesn't want to be left out.

She can't believe it when they tell her they're planning a holiday. She thinks it's her mother's idea but her father tells her it was his. He tells her they've finally finished paying off the hospital bills and they want to go away. Relax for a while. They want her to come of course but she can't imagine leaving. She says she won't go but they say she has to. They say she's too young to stay home alone. She points out that she's almost the same age her sister was when she left home but her parents say that's different and she can't see how.

He makes her try it in their room. At first he isn't going to have any but she can see he wants to so she pushes him a little, it doesn't take much, and he agrees. She feels nervous when she sees the needle. Her fear grows as she watches him prepare it for her. She thinks he's moving too fast because suddenly the needle is on her arm and then she's watching it go in and then it hits. And when it hits she stops thinking at all.

He likes the drug. She can tell by the way he talks about it the next day. She thinks she likes it too. She imagines now she's tried the drug that things will go back to the way they were. Titch and Pete will start inviting them wherever they go and she'll feel part of a group again.

Sometimes it's like that but most of the time it's not. Something has changed and she's not quite sure what it is. There's a new group of people. The parties are smaller. She likes it when it's just the four of them or just her and Steve best. She doesn't care about the parties anymore. She wonders if she ever did. But it's rarely the four of them now and she's not sure why.

She waits for her outside the supermarket. She waits until half an hour past her finishing time but her sister doesn't come out. She goes back the following day and waits again. Her sister appears this time. She asks her about yesterday and she just says she wasn't feeling well. It makes her worried. She questions her, hearing her mother's voice coming out of her mouth.

Why? Why weren't you well?
I just didn't feel well.

She leaves it alone.

They want to go away for a while.

So?
It's not right, not without you
I don't care.

I do. Why don't you come home?

I have another home now. I don't want to live there. I don't care what they do.

There's nothing she can say. She watches her sister walk away like she always does but today she follows her. Her sister never suspects. Never looks back. She follows her to her house, a shabby looking place with car parts and rubbish scattered over the dead front lawn. She watches her sister walk inside. She wonders what the house is like on the inside and what her boyfriend looks like as she walks back to her own home.

Weeks go by when they don't even use the drug. And then it's maybe a week. And then she notices it's just her not using it very often because when she gets home from work she can see it in him and she becomes jealous. She's pushing groceries over the counter all day and he's just lying around. She wishes she could just throw away her job with the same lack of concern he did but she can't. They need the money now. His dole isn't enough. She doesn't think they could survive without her job.

They fire her anyway. She takes one sick day too many and they ask her to leave. You can't take sick days when you work at a supermarket. They don't operate like that. She tries to think how many days she's taken off. It can't be that many. But obviously it's enough. That and her uniform, which she never seems to have time to wash these days, let alone iron. As she walks back to the house she wonders how Steve will react and how they're going to pay the rent.

Steve doesn't care about her losing her job. He says it's just more time they can spend together. He takes her to the dole office and shows her how to fill in the forms. She thinks it will be hard. She thinks they will question her about being too young and why she left home. But they don't really care about her there. They look over her forms, tell her a few things and then she leaves. Steve smiles at her.

See? Nothing to it.

But she worries there will never be enough money now.

She thought she would look for another job straight away but Steve encourages her to take some time off. Relax for a while. Like he's been doing. She knows he has no intention of looking for another job and she begins to wonder if, in a few weeks, she'll start to feel the same way.

She's surprised when her sister knocks on the door. So surprised she lets her in and introduces her to Steve. Steve says hi to her but then goes into their room. To let them talk. She can see her sister is disgusted by the mess in the house but she forces herself not to care. She'd planned to clean up now she wasn't working but she hasn't got around to it yet. She doesn't ask her sister how she knew where she was. Instead she asks her for money. She's surprised the words come out of her mouth but she can't stop them. Her sister gives her everything she has. It's not much but she promises to get her more. She doesn't know why her sister is willing to give her money but she takes it and as a way to thank her, tells her to drop by any time.

She doesn't tell her parents about her visit with her sister. She keeps it to herself. Sometimes she thinks about telling a teacher, asking for advice but she knows what the advice would be and she knows her sister wouldn't want to hear it so she keeps it to herself. She tells herself she's just waiting for an opportunity. An opportunity to get her sister back. She starts lying to her parents, taking money from them and saving it for the next time she sees her sister. She worries about the holiday. Who will look out for her while she's away?

Her dreams begin to blend with her reality. Sometimes she doesn't know if she's awake or asleep. Her dreams and her life blend together to become one big mess. She tells him, my dreams are real. He says cool but she knows he isn't hearing her. In her dreams she's eloquent, full of words and thoughts that she explains to the people around her. She tells them what's going on, what's going to happen. She tells them, my dreams are real.

They stop paying rent. Not just her and Steve but Titch and Pete too. No one pays any rent. She doesn't know who made the decision. They just stopped. Luke and Dave have moved out. She asked where they were once. Titch told her they moved out a month ago. She didn't even notice.

She knows they'll be kicked out soon but until then they're still in the house. Waiting for it to happen. Titch and Pete are looking for somewhere else to live and she supposes that she and Steve should be doing the same thing. But they're concentrating on other things now.

She tries to push the memories of her elder daughter away. She tries to forget the pain and guilt she feels. In her mind she concentrates on making her memories smaller, shrinking them down and putting them away. The memories don't hurt her like that. Not like they hurt when they're large and real. It takes a lot of thought, a lot of concentration to get her memories under control. As soon as she stops concentrating they blow back up to their original size and she becomes lost in them. She thinks she won't have the memories around her when they go on holiday. She thinks her mind will be full of the new things she is seeing. Of course she is wrong. She becomes relaxed on holiday and the memories unfold themselves, larger and stronger than ever.

Sometimes when she looks at him she doesn't know who he is. Usually she doesn't really look at him at all. She just knows he's there. Almost a part of her. He's all she has now and she wonders if she takes him for granted. Sometimes when she looks at him and doesn't know who he is she gets scared. He's all she has and she doesn't know who he is. She never tells him this. Instead she remembers how they met and all the nice things he said to her. She hangs onto him because he is all she's got.

There are times when she thinks she's beautiful. Times when she looks at her body and sees it as right. She enjoys these times. Looks forward to them and tries to make them last. But then there are times when she looks at her body and it has never looked more wrong. When she can see how fat she is and her skin feels dirty and sweaty. She showers at these times. Showers and showers but the shower is mouldy and the towel is damp and she can never feel clean. There are other times. Times when her body doesn't even seem to exist. She thinks these times are the best.

It comes as a relief when they are thrown out of the house. They are no longer waiting for something to happen. Titch and Pete have somewhere to go and disappear quickly. They haven't even talked about what they would do or where they would go. They take Mark's old mattress out of the house and drag it to a nearby squat because they can't think of anything else to do. The squat is full of people and arguments. They don't care. They stake their corner, lie down and try to think about what to do next.

Her glory has gone now. Like the fat girl. There's no more glory telling her what to do and who to be. No more fat girl whispering in her ear. No more dreams in the reflection of shop windows. She wonders if her glory has gone because she doesn't need it any more. Or if she does need it and just lost it on the way, like she lost everything else, like she lost the fat girl. She wonders where they've gone. Whose ear they're whispering in now.

When they get back from their holiday she goes to her sister's house as soon as she can get away. She panics when she sees they aren't there. She has no idea where to look or if there's anyone she can ask, so she walks. She walks around the neighbourhood as often as she can. Hoping she might see her walking down the street or waiting at the bus stop. The longer she looks the more worried she becomes. She starts to ask people on the street. Anyone who looks like they're the right age.

That's how she finds out about the squat. That's how she finds her sister. Sitting on a dirty mattress in a dirty building. Her boyfriend sleeping beside her. She does what she can. She tries to talk to her about finding somewhere else to live, about eating, about coming home, just for a shower and a clean bed, just for a night. It makes her feel old talking to her sister like this even though her sister doesn't listen. She didn't really expect that she would. She gives her the money she has saved and promises to be back. She watches her sister take the money and nod her head but she's not sure she's hearing anything.

She tries to make the money last but it slips between her fingers. She stopped watching how much Steve was using a while ago. She became more interested in what was going into her arm. But as she concentrates on trying to make the money last she realises how expensive he has become. She doesn't say anything. She wouldn't know what to say. She can't not give him money. She can't tell him to slow down while she's greedily doing the same thing. She doesn't even go back to watching. She just goes back to concentrating on herself.

That's why it takes her a while to realise what's happening. She doesn't notice the shaking, the sweating. It's only when she smells the vomit that she realises something is wrong. He loses consciousness and she just looks at him. She doesn't know what to do. She feels other people in the squat shaking her. They pick her up and make her walk. Pick him up and help her drag him to the hospital. No one can afford a taxi. They walk.

When they finally get to the hospital they leave her there, holding Steve, waiting for someone to come and help him. She tries to remember how they met and who he is. She tries to answer their questions. They take him away from her and tell her to come back in the morning. She nods her head and leaves the hospital. She walks slowly back to the squat because she doesn't know where else to go.

She doesn't go back to the hospital in the morning. She doesn't go anywhere. She stays on their mattress and waits for something to happen. She thinks about Steve, and Titch, and Mandy, and Cherie. She thinks about Samantha and her family and what it was like when she was in the hospital. She thinks about her glory and the fat girl and wonders if they really left her or if they're still there. Somewhere inside of her. She gets tired of thinking.

In her dream her sister appears. She watches her walk through the squat until she is standing beside the mattress. Her sister takes her hand and pulls her to her feet. She doesn't ask where they're going. She just holds onto the hand. Because there's nothing else left to do.

I am standing. Standing on the edge of a cliff.

Below me is the ocean. It's so far away that it looks like a toy, harmless, as it falls on the rocks below.

Behind me are my parents and sister. They're sitting on a blanket. Eating.

But I am standing. Standing on the edge of a cliff.

I STARTED CRYING MONDAY
Laurene Kelly

"a commendable first novel"
                    – *Notable Australian Children's Books 2000*

Fourteen-year-old Julie starts crying on Monday when things go badly at school. Worse is to come.

ISBN 1-875559-78-7

THE CROWDED BEACH
Laurene Kelly

Julie's youthful concerns are swept aside by a tragedy that splits her family. She and her brother Toby must begin a new life in Sydney, a city that is sometimes exciting, often overwhelming and always different to the only home she has ever known. The sequel to acclaimed *I Started Crying Monday*.

ISBN 1-876756-06-3

THRILLER AND ME
Merrilee Moss

Angelica's twelve – and no angel, as she says herself. Now her Dad has disappeared and life is even stranger than usual. She sets out to discover where he has gone and why. A humourous and thoughtful story dealing with issues of sexuality and family.
ISBN 1-875843-05-1

KICK THE TIN
Doris Kartinyeri

"[Kick the Tin] is a story of courage and survival, power-fully demonstrating how the human spirit can soar despite all the injuries and injustices which threaten to drag it down."

– Lowitja O'Donoghue

ISBN 1-875559-95-7

THE ANGER OF AUBERGINES
Bulbul Sharma

Food as a passion, a gift, a means of revenge, even a source of power.

ISBN 1-876756-01-2

FAR AND BEYON'
Unity Dow

A powerful coming of age story set in contemporary Africa. Unity Dow is the first female High Court judge in Botswana, and has previously been prominent as a human rights activist.

"Dow writes this world the way men and women in her country sing – with a zest fed by connection to the earth and to a shared past."

– Morag Fraser, *The Age*

ISBN 1-876756-07-1

POEMS FROM THE MADHOUSE
Sandy Jeffs

"This is disturbing but quite wonderful poetry, because of its clarity, its humour, its imagery, and the insights it gives us into being human, being mad, being sane. I read and read – and was profoundly moved.

– Anne Deveson

ISBN 1-876756-03-9

BIRD AND OTHER WRITINGS ON EPILEPSY
Susan Hawthorne

"Susan Hawthorne has accepted her gift: the intense realisation of coming to life. This is what her book offers."

– Judith Rodriguez

ISBN 1-875559-88-4

THE SPINIFEX QUIZ BOOK
Susan Hawthorne

Australian Awards for Excellence in Educational Publishing, 1993

"*The Spinifex Quiz Book* is funny, instructive, entertaining, and inspiring... use it alone or in school. I recommend it wholeheartedly."

– Senta Trömel-Plötz, *Virginia*

"It should be compulsory reading in every Year 10 class in Australia."

–Alison Coates, *ABC Radio*

ISBN 1-875559-15-9

If you would like to know more about Spinifex Press
write for a free catalogue or visit our website

SPINIFEX PRESS
PO Box 212 North Melbourne
Victoria 3051 Australia
<http://www.spinifexpress.com.au>